T0654666

John Alexander Macdonell

A Sketch of the Life of the Honourable And Right Reverend

Alexander Macdonell

John Alexander Macdonell

A Sketch of the Life of the Honourable And Right Reverend Alexander Macdonell

ISBN/EAN: 9783744725415

Printed in Europe, USA, Canada, Australia, Japan

Cover: Foto ©Raphael Reischuk / pixelio.de

More available books at **www.hansebooks.com**

A SKETCH OF THE LIFE

— OF —

THE HONOURABLE AND RIGHT REVEREND

ALEXANDER MACDONELL,

CHAPLAIN OF THE GLENGARRY FENCIBLE OR BRITISH HIGHLAND REGIMENT,
FIRST CATHOLIC BISHOP OF UPPER CANADA, AND A MEMBER OF
THE LEGISLATIVE COUNCIL OE THE PROVINCE.

— BY —

J. A. MACDONELL,

OF GREENFIELD.

ALEXANDRIA :
Printed at the Office of The Glengarrian,
1890.

To the Right Honourable

SIR JOHN MACDONALD, G.C.B.

My Dear Sir John,

I send you the advance sheets of a little sketch I have written of the life of your old friend Bishop Macdonell. It is, however, as you will observe, largely a compilation of such papers as I have been able to collect as were written by him in his lifetime, and of circumstances in his career which are stated by others.

Those who were friends of the Bishop are now necessarily few. He died in 1840—as you remember—a half century ago. The incidents which I recall will, I hope, have some interest for you and others who recollect him and appreciated his great worth ; while the example which he set may well be emulated by those of younger generations.

He feared God and served his Sovereign, and his motto was peace and good will among men of all creeds, AND OUR COUNTRY FOR OURSELVES.

It is because you inculcate the same doctrine into the minds and hearts of your Countrymen that they follow you with such devotion, and will follow you to the end.

Yours always,

J. A. MACDONELL.

Glengarry, July, 1890.

THE HONOURABLE AND RIGHT REVEREND
ALEXANDER MACDONELL,

CHAPLAIN OF THE GLENGARRY FENCIBLE OR BRITISH HIGHLAND REGIMENT, FIRST CATHOLIC BISHOP OF UPPER CANADA, AND A MEMBER OF THE LEGISLATIVE COUNCIL OF THE PROVINCE.

My friend, the Chevalier Macdonell, recently Vice-Consul of France at Toronto, states that this distinguished man was born in Glen Urquhart, on the borders of Loch Ness, Inverness-shire, Scotland, on the 17th July, 1762. As to the place of his birth, however, as not infrequently happens, some doubt exists.* Few men were in a better position to speak authoritatively on the subject than the Bishop's grand-nephew, Mr. John Allan Macdonell, J.P., of St. Raphael's, and in a memorandum given to me by him some years since, it is stated that the Bishop was born at Inchlaggan in Glengarry, Scotland, in 1760. I am now unable, owing to Mr. Macdonell's state of health, to obtain from him the source of his information. It may or may not be traditionary, but I am free to state that it accords with the views of most of the people in Glengarry to whom I have spoken on the subject.

Unfortunately, the greater portion of the Bishop's papers are lost, I fear irretrievably, and excepting what found its way into print from his own pen during his lifetime, facts con-

---

*A striking instance in point is that of the Duke of Wellington ; although the son of an Irish Peer, the Earl of Mornington, it is uncertain whether he was born in Dublin or at Dungan Castle, Meath, nor is the date of his birth certain. It was in the spring of 1769, in the latter end of April or beginning of May.

cerning him especially personally, now largely rest on tradition. But the exact date and exact place of his birth are of no very great importance. It is of the great use he made of the life God gave him, of the talents a nd great parts with which he was so liberally endowed, of his usefulness to the Church of his forefathers, of his stalwart loyalty to his Sovereign, of his services to his adopted country, and of the all-abiding love he bore his Scottish fellow-countrymen—that we have to do.

His parents were respectable people of Glengarry's clan—of much the same class and walk in life as those of that other great Scottish-Canadian of his own time, his colleague in the Legislative Council and intimate friend of many years, Bishop Strachan, the head and front in this Province of the Anglican Church, as Bishop Macdonell was of that to which he belonged. They were people who were unable to give their children any great advantages in a worldly point of view, but who instilled into them from the cradle those great principles which became of themselves a heritage of inestimable value, and of which both so largely availed themselves to the benefit of the flock over which were respectively called upon in time to become the shepherds in a common and far distant country.

Being destined for the Church, and there being no Catholic Colleges in Scotland at the time, Mr. Macdonell was at an early age first sent to the Scottish College in Paris, and subsequently to the Scots' College at Valladolid in Spain. While in Paris, the students at his Seminary were on one occasion brought from their peaceful retreat by some revolutionary enthusiasts and forced to dance around a Liberty Pole. Mr. Macdonell, who in early life, as in more mature age, was an ardent Royalist, was much shocked at such an outrageous proceeding, and with a ready wit bound a handkerchief around his knee and feigning lameness, thus managed to escape the threatened indignity.

He was ordained Priest at Valladolid, in Spain, on February 16th, 1787, and on leaving there returned to Scotland, and was stationed as a Missionary Priest in the Braes of Lochaber, where he remained for several years.

Of the events of the following years in which he took an active part and until his arrival in Canada, we fortunately have his own account published in the Canadian Literary Magazine of April, 1833, Volume 1, page 3, et seq. After explaining how, consequent upon the abolition of the feudal system of clanship which had obtained from time immemorial, and had been based upon the mutual interest of Chieftain and clansmen, by the influence and consequence in proportion to the number of his followers if afforded the former—and the protection and support it gave to the latter—the " bleak and barren mountains of the north," which had previously raised MEN. had been converted into sheep walks, and the suffering thus necessarily entailed upon the people—their utter misery in fact—he proceeds :—"It was in this conjuncture that the writer of these pages, then a missionary on the borders of the Counties of Inverness and Perth, in the highest inhabited parts of the Highlands of Scotland, affected by the distressed state of his countrymen, and hearing that an emigrant vessel which had sailed from the Island of Barra, one of the Hebrides, had been wrecked and had put into Greenock, where she landed her passengers in the most helpless and destitute situation—repaired in the spring of 1792 to Glasgow. Having secured an introduction to several of the professors of the University and to the principal manufacturers of that city, he proposed to the latter that he should induce the Highlanders who had been turned out of their farms, and those lately escaped from the shipwreck, to enter into their works if they (the manufacturers) would but encourage them, and this they readily promised to do upon very liberal terms. There were two serious obstacles, however, to the usefulness of the Highlanders : the one that they did not understand the English language, the other that a large portion of them were Roman Catholics. The excitement raised by Lord George Gordon about Catholics twelve years before, when the Catholic chapels of Edinburgh and Glasgow, and the clergymen's houses, were burned, had not yet subsided ; and a strong and rancorous feeling against the professors of the Catholic religion still remained amongst the lower orders of the people of Glasgow ; so much so, indeed, that no Catholic clergyman could with safety reside there from the time of the burning of the chapels to the period we are now speaking of. The manufacturers represented to the missionary that although perfectly willing themselves to afford the Catholics all the countenance and protection in their power, yet, as the Penal laws still remained in full force against them, they could not be answerable for the consequences in the event of evil-designed persons assailing or annoying them ; and they represented that the danger was still greater to a Catholic clergyman, who was subject not only to the insult and abuse of the rabble, but to be arraigned before a Court of Justice. To this the missionary replied that although the letter of the law militated against Catholics, the spirit of it was greatly mitigated, and that if they would but assure the Highlanders of their protection, he himself would take his chance of the severity of the law and the fanaticism of the people, and accompany the Highlanders to the manufactories, in order to serve them in the double capacity of interpreter and clergyman ; for the missionary saw that it was a notorious fact that Catholics following the dictates of their religion and restrained by its morality made faithful and industrious servants ; but discarding those ties and obligations, they became vicious and unprincipled.

" The manufacturers, appearing much pleased with this proposal, offered every protection and encouragement in their power to himself and followers. Accordingly, with the approbation of his Bishop, he took up his residence in Glasgow in June, 1792, and in the course of a few months procured employment for upwards of 600 Highlanders.

" On the few occasions previous to this, that a Priest had officiated in Glasgow, he was obliged to hold his meetings up two or three pairs of stairs, and to station at the door a sturdy Irishman or Highlander armed with a bludgeon to overawe the intruders who might attempt to disturb the service. But the missionary, by the advice of one of the most influential Presbyterians of the city, * opened his chapel to the street and did not close the door during the service. Two respectable members of the congregation attended to show any decent persons, attracted thither by curiosity, into a seat ; and several who thus came were repeatedly heard to say that this was not Popery at all, although the principal tenets of the Catholic religion were taught and explained both in English and Gaelic ; and because they saw neither pictures nor images, and the Mass was said early in the morning, before those who might be

---

* Dr. Porteous, a nephew, by marriage, of Sir John Moore.

disposed to give annoyance were up, and who, being of the lower class of laborers and tradesmen, generally spent the Saturday evenings in a tavern and Sunday mornings in bed.

"For two years the manufacturers went on with astonishing prosperity and success, but in the year 1794 the principles of the French revolution spreading rapidly over Great Britain, and meeting with the warmest abettors in the manufacturing districts, the English Government found it necessary to adopt measures to check its progress and to prevent intercourse between the two countries.

"War was at length proclaimed between England and France. The export of British manufactures to the continent was stopped ; the credit of the manufacturers was checked ; their works were almost at a stand ; frequent bankruptcies ensued ; a general dismissal of laboring hands took place, and misery and distress overtook those thus suddenly thrown out of employ.

"Among the sufferers were the poor Highlanders above mentioned. Unaccustomed to hard labor and totally ignorant of the English language, they became more helpless and destitute than any other class of the whole community.

Raising of the Glengarry Fencible, or British Highland Regiment.

"At this crisis the missionary conceived the idea of getting these unfortunate Highlanders embodied as a Catholic corps in His Majesty's service, with his young Chief, Macdonell of Glengarry, for their Colonel. Having procured a meeting of the Catholics at Fort Augustus, in February, 1794, a loyal address was drawn up to the King, offering to raise a Catholic corps, under the command of the young Chieftain, who, together with John Fletcher, Esq., of Dunans, proceeded as a deputation to London with the address, which was most graciously received by the King. The manufacturers of Glasgow furnished them with the most ample and honorable testimonials of the good conduct of the Highlanders during the time they had been at their works, and strongly recommended that they should be employed in the service of their country. A Letter of Service was accordingly issued to raise the first Glengarry Fencible Regiment as a Catholic corps, being the first that was raised as such since the Reformation.

" The missionary, although contrary to the then existing law, was gazetted as Chaplain of the regiment. Four or five regiments which had been raised in Scotland, having refused to extend their services to England, and having mutinied when they were ordered to march, the Glengarry Fencibles, by the persuation of their Chaplain, offered to extend their services to any part of Great Britain or Ireland, or even to the islands of Jersey or Guernsey. This offer was very acceptable to the Government, since it formed a precedent to all Fencible corps that were raised after this period. The regiment, having been embodied in June, 1795, soon afterwards embarked for Guernsey, and remained there until the summer of 1798.

" Sir Sidney Smith having taken possession of the small island of St. Marcou, in the mouth of Cherbourg Harbor, the Glengarries offered to garrison that post, but the capture of that gallant officer and of the much lamented Captain Wright, who was first tortured and then put to death in a French prison because he would not take a commission in the French navy, prevented the enterprise from taking place.

" In the summer of 1798 the rebellion broke out in Ireland, and the Glengarry regiment was ordered to that country. Landing at Ballenack, they marched from thence to Waterford, and from Waterfore to New Ross the same day. At the former place a trifling circumstance occurred which afforded no small surprise to some and no slight ridicule to others, while at the same time it showed the simplicity of the Highlanders and their ignorance of the ways of the world. The soldiers who received billet money on their entrance in the town returned it on their being ordered to march the same evening to New Ross for the purpose of reinforcing Gen. Johnson, who was surrounded, and, in a manner, besieged by the rebels.

" The next day Gen. Johnson attacked and dislodged the rebels from Laggan Hill, who, after a very faint resistance, retreated to Vinegar Hill. The Chaplain, upon this and all other occasions, accompanied the regiment to the field with the view of preventing the men from plundering or committing any act of cruelty upon the country people. The command of the town of New Ross devolved on Col. Macdonell, and the Chaplain found the jail and court house crowded with wounded rebels, whose lives had been spared, but who had been totally neglected. Their wounds had never been dressed, nor any sustenance been given to them since the day of the battle. Col. Macdonell, on being informed of their miserable condition, ordered the surgeon of his regiment to attend them, and every possible relief was offered to the wretched sufferers. From New Ross the regiment was ordered to Kilkenny, and from thence to Hackett's Town, in the County of Wicklow, to reduce a body of rebels and deserters, who had taken possession of the the neighboring mountains, under the command of the rebel chiefs, Holt and Dwyer.

"The village of Hackett's Town had been entirely consumed to ashes, partly by the insurgents and partly by the military. Deprived of this shelter, the troops were compelled to live under tents the greater part of the winter, and the Chaplain considered it his duty to share their privations and sufferings.

"Colonel Macdonell, who now commanded the Brigade, which consisted of the Glengarries, two companies of the Eighty-Ninth Regiment of Foot, two companies of Lord Darlington's Fencible Cavalry and several companies of the Yeomanry, finding that the rebels made a practice of descending from the mountains in the night time to the hamlets in the valleys for the purpose of plunder, adopted a plan of getting the troops under arms about midnight and marching them from the camp in two divisions without fife or drum. One division was ordered to gain the summits of the mountains, the other to scour the inhabited parts of the country; so that the rebels, in attempting to regain their footsteps, found themselves entrapped between two fires. The Chaplain never failed to accompany one or the other of these divisions, and was the means of saving the lives of, and preserving for legal trial, many prisoners, whom the yeomanry would, but for his interference, have put to immediate death.

"The Catholic chapels in many of those parts had been turned into stables for the yeomanry cavalry, but the Chaplain, when he came, caused them to be cleaned out and restored to their proper use. He also invited the terrified inhabitants and clergy to resume their accustomed worship, and labored not in vain to restore tranquility and peace to the people, pursuading them that if they behaved quietly and peacefully the Government would protect Catholics as well as Protestants, and impressing upon their minds that the Government having entrusted arms to the hands of the Glengarry Highlanders, who were Roman Catholics, was a proof that it was not inimical to them on account of their religion. These exhortations, together with the restoration of divine service in the chapels, the strict discipline enforced by Colonel Macdonell, and the repression of the licentiousness of the yeomanry, served in a great measure to restore confidence to the people, to allay feelings of dissatisfaction and to extinguish the embers of rebellion wherever the Glengarry Regiment served.

"The Highlanders, whom the rebels called 'the Devil's Blood-hounds,' both on account of their dress and their habit of climbing and traversing the mountains, had greatly the advantage of the insurgents in every recountre, so much so that in a few months their force was reduced from a thousand to a few scores. Holt, seeing his numbers so fast diminishing, surrendered to Lord Powerscourt, and was transported to Botany Bay. Dwyer, after almost his whole party had been killed or taken, was at length surprised in a house with his few remaining followers by a party of the Glengarries. Here he defended himself and killed some of his pursuers, till the house being set on fire, he was shot while endeavoring to make his escape, stark naked, through the flames.

"The Marquess Cornwallis, Lord-Lieutenant of Ireland, commander of the forces, was so well pleased with the services of the Glengarry Fencibles that he advised the Government to have the regiment augmented. In furtherance of this plan, the Chaplain was despatched to London with recommendations from every General under whose command the corps had served in Guernsey or in Ireland, to procure the proposed augmentation and to settle on the terms. Previous to his departure from Dublin, the measure of a legislative union between Great Britain and Ireland had been brought into the Irish Parliament and miscarried. The Catholic Bishops and Catholic nobles of Ireland having assembled in Dublin to discuss this subject, came to a determination favorable to the views of Government, and communicated their sentiments to the Chaplain, authorizing him to impart them to the Ministry. The Chaplain did so accordingly in his first interview with the Right Honourable Henry Dundas, afterwards Lord Melville, but that statesman considered the Chaplain's information incorrect, and insinuated that the intention of the Irish Catholic dignitaries and nobility was quite contrary to what was stated.

" He also privately informed Sir John Cox Hippesley, who accompanied the Chaplain to the Secretary of State's office, that by a despatch received through that day's mail from Lord Castlereagh, the Secretary of State for Ireland, he was informed that the purpose of the meeting of the Catholics was to counteract the measures of the Government. This the Chaplain took the liberty to deny, and offered to prove his assertion to the satisfaction of Mr. Dundas by being allowed time to refer to the Catholic meeting at Dublin. He accordingly wrote to Colonel Macdonell, whom he had left in that city, and received by return of post an answer from Viscount Kenmare, contradicting in toto the assertions of Viscount Castlereagh. On this occasion the Government papers indulged in severe reflections upon the conduct of the Irish Catholics. The Chaplain requested that they should be contradicted, which was done very reluctantly and not until he had threatened to have the truth published in the Opposition papers. The correspondence on that subject is now in his possession.

" The proposed augmentation, however, did not take place. The views of government were altered, and instead of augmenting the Fencible Corps, they gave commissions in the regiments of the line to those officers of the Fencibles who could bring a certain number of volunteers with them.

" The Glengarry Fencibles were afterwards employed in the mountains and other parts of Conomaragh, where some of the most desperate rebels had taken refuge, and where the embers of rebellion continued longest unextinguished. The Chaplain was their constant attendant down to the year 1802, when at the short peace of Amiens, the whole of the Scotch Fencibles were disbanded."

I have obtained a list of the officers of this regiment from an army list of 1798. The regiment was stationed at Kilkenny at the time. It will be observed that Colonel Macdonald is named as Colonel, Glengarry being in charge of the Brigade.

Colonel—Donald Macdonald.
Lieutenant-Colonel—Charles McLean.
Major—Alexander Macdonell.

Captains.

Archibald McLachlan,	James Macdonald,
Donald Macdonald,	Archibald Macdonell,
Ranald Macdonell.	Roderick Macdonald,

Hugh Beaton.

Captain-Lieutenant and Captain—Alexander Macdonell.

Lieutenants.

John Macdonald,	James McNab,
Ronald Macdonald,	D. McIntyre,
Archibald McLellan,	Donald Chisholm,
James Macdonell,	Allan McNab.

Ensigns.

Alexander Macdonell,	Donald Maclean,
John Macdonald,	Archibald Macdonell,
Charles Macdonald,	Alexander Macdonell,
Donald Macdonell,	Andrew Macdonell,

Francis Livingstone.

Adjutant—Donald Macdonell.
Quarter-Master—Alexander Macdonell.
Surgeon—Alexander Macdonell.

Taken as a whole, the names seem to be somewhat Scotch, and to savor, as did those of the men, of the clan whose suaicheantas was the heather !

I may mention that this is but one of the twenty-six Scottish regiments, almost all Highland, enumerated in the army list of 1798, though a young essayist has gravely assured us that the finer qualities and instincts of the men of that and previous generations had been dwarfed by long subjection to despotism of their chiefs, and that even their physique had degenerated under oppression, and that it required years and another climate and changed surroundings to counteract the stunting influences of centuries.

THE CHAPLAIN'S NEGOTIATIONS WITH THE BRITISH GOVERNMENT ON BEHALF OF THE DISBANDED REGIMENT.

" The Highlanders now found themselves in the same destitute situation as they were in when first introduced into the manufactories of Glasgow. Struck with their forlorn condition, the Chaplain, at his own expense, proceeded to London to represent their situation to the Government and to endeavour to induce ministers to lend them assistance to emigrate to Upper Canada. He was introduced to the Right Honourable Charles Yorke, Secretary at War, and by him to Mr. Addington, the Premier. The latter, on account of the testimonials which the Chaplain presented to him of the good conduct of the regiment during the whole of their service, signed by the different general officers under whose command they had been, directed that a sum of money should be paid to the Chaplain, out of the Military Chaplain's fund in lieu of half pay, which could not be granted to him without forming a precedent to other Chaplains of Fencible Corps ; and this favor was conferred upon him at the recommendation of His Royal Highness the Duke of York, then Commander in Chief, on account of his having constantly attended the regiment when every other regimental Chaplain had retired upon five shillings a day, by virtue of an order issued from the War Office in 1798. Mr. Addington requested the Chaplain to state to him, in writing, the cause of the frequent emigrations from the Highlands of Scotland. The Chaplain complied with his request in a series of letters, on the perusal of which Mr. Addington expressed his deep regret that so brave and faithful a portion of His Majesty's subjects, who were always found ready at the call of Government, and from whom no murmurs or discontents were ever heard, even under the most trying and distressing circumstances, should be compelled to quit their native soil by the harsh treatment of their landlords, and to transfer their allegiance to the United States, whither the emigration had been flowing previous to this period.

"Mr. Addington added that the loss of so many Highlanders was one of the circumstances which had given him the greatest uneasiness during his administration, and that nothing would give him greater satisfaction than to convince them of the friendly feelings and kind intentions of Government towards them by putting them in the way of acquiring, in a few years, prosperity, and even wealth, with which they might return and live in ease and independence in their native land. He then proposed to the Chaplain to send a colony of those Highlanders with whom he was connected to the island of Trinidad, which was then first ceded to the British Empire ; and to give a farm of eighty acres of land to every head of a family, and money out of the the the treasury to purchase four slaves for every farm ; a larger proportion of land and slaves to such gentlemen who would accompany the colony, and to the Chaplain as large a salary as he could reasonably demand. Mr. Addington also offered to send a surgeon and a schoolmaster, with salaries from Government, to the new colony, and, to remove the difficulties which the Chaplain had stated in regard to the unhealthiness of a tropical climate and the propensity of Highlanders to drink ardent spirits, undertook to furnish the colony with as much wine as the Chaplain and surgeon should consider necessary for the preservation of the general health for three years, also sufficient vinegar wherewith to wash their habitations for the same period ; after which it might be supposed that the constitution of the settlers would become inured to the climate.

" For these liberal and advantageous offers the Chaplain could not but feel grateful to Mr. Addington, but while he thanked him for kind intentions towards his countrymen, he assured him that no consideration on earth would induce him to prevail upon Highlanders to reside in the unhealthy climate of the West Indies, or reconcile to his conscience the bitter reflection of his being the cause of making a woman or a child a widow or an orphan.

" Mr. Addington seemed greatly surprised and disappointed at this expression of the Chaplain's sentiments, and demanded in what other way he could serve the Highlanders. He was answered that what they expected and wished was to be assisted in emigrating to

Upper Canada, where several of their friends had already settled themselves.

" 'The Chaplain proceeded to state that if this assistance were tendered upon a more extensive scale, it would allay the irritated feelings entertained by the Highlanders against their landlords, whose cruel conduct was identified with the system and operations of Government. Moreover, the Scotch, quitting their country in this exasperated state of mind, and settling in the United States, readily imbibed republican principles and a determined antipathy against the British Government ; whereas by diverting the tide of emigration into the British colonies, their population would be increased by settlers retaining British principles, British feelings and an attachment towards their native country, not only undiminished, but even increased by the parental conduct of the Government towards them.

" Mr. Addington then offered to lend some assistance to the Chaplain to convey his adherents to the sea coast of Nova Scotia, New Brunswick or Cape Breton, but assured him that His Majesty's Government considered the hold they had of Upper Canada so slender and so precarious that a person in his situation would not be justified in putting his hand in the public purse to assist British subjects to emigrate to that colony. The Chaplain, however, adhered to his first resolution of conducting his countrymen to Upper Canada, and Mr. Addington procured for him an order (with the Sign Manual) to the Lieutenant-Governor of Upper Canada to grant two hundred acres of land to every one of the Highlanders who should arrive in the Province.

" No sooner was it known that this order had been given by the Secretary for the Colonies than the Highland landlords and proprietors took the alarm, considering the order as an allurement to entice from the country their vassals and dependents.

" Sir John McPherson, Sir Archibald Macdonald (the Lord Chief Baron of the Exchequer in England), the late Mr. Charles Grant, one of the directors of the East India Company and M.P. for the County of Inverness, with other gentlemen connected with the Highlands, and even the Earl of Moira, then commanding the forces in North Britain, endeavored to dissuade the Chaplain from his purpose, and promised to procure a pension for him provided he would separate himself from the Highlanders whom he had promised to take to Canada, and that the amount of the pension should be in proportion to the number he should prevail upon to stay at home.

"So anxious were these gentlemen to keep the Highlanders at home that they applied to the Prince of Wales, and by His Royal Highness' sanction, Sir Thomas Tyrrwhit, the Prince's agent, sent for the Chaplain to Carlton House for the purpose of prevailing upon him to induce the intending emigrants to settle on the waste lands of the County of Cornwall, under the patronage and protection of His Royal Highness. This the Chaplain also declined, and in concert with Major Archibald Campbell, then on the staff of General Pulteney, now* Lieutenant-Governor of New Brunswick, proposed a plan of organizing a Military emigration, to be composed of the soldiers of the several Scotch Fencible regiments just then disbanded, and sending them over to Upper Canada for the double purpose of forming an internal defence and settling the country. It was requested that a certain portion of land should be granted to every man after a service of five years, or on his furnishing a substitute; so that the same force might always be kept up and the settlement of the country go on. It was considered that this plan would prevent the frequent desertion of His Majesty's troops to the United States; would make these military settlers interested in the defence of the Province, and be a prodigious saving of transport of troops in the event of a war with the United States.

"Several distinguished officers appeared anxious to join this military emigration, and the scheme was nearly matured, when Mr. Addington found himself under the necessity of resigning the Premiership, and Pitt and Dundas returned to office.

"The war was soon after renewed, and the Scotch landlords combined to keep their people at home.

"Most of these gentlemen had received commissions from the Government to raise levies, and were, of course, anxious to fulfil their engagements. Seeing that so many thousands of their poor countrymen who had been let loose in the country in a state of destitution, had no other alternative, if prevented from emigrating,

---

* At the time the Bishop wrote the narrative, 1833.

than to enter the army, they procured an act of Parliament to impose certain restrictions and regulations on vessels carrying out emigrants to the colonies. By those regulations, a vessel could not get her clearance from the Custom House if she had more than one passenger, even an infant, for every two tons of the registered burden of the ship—although the transport regulations for carrying troops to the East and West Indies allowed a ton and a half for every soldier, even without reckoning women and children; another clause was that the provision should be inspected and certified, that a pound of salt beef or pork and a pound and a half of flour or of hard biscuit should be found on board as the daily provision for every man, woman and child for the space of three months. A third clause was that a vessel carrying emigrants from any part in Great Britain and Ireland to the colonies should be provided with a surgeon, who should have his diploma from Surgeons' Hall in London, from Edinburgh University or Trinity College, Dublin. A diploma from any other college or university in Great Britain would not qualify him for this charge. Several other clauses similar to the above were contained in this act, and all under the specious pretext of humanity and tender benevolence towards the emigrants, and, forsooth, to prevent the imposition of those who were employed in chartering vessels to carry emigrants to the colonies, who were designated by the Scotch lairds, dealers in white slaves; yet, by the operations of this merciful act of Parliament, an emigrant could not pay the passage of himself, his wife and four children under eight years of age for a less sum than £84!

"Alexander Hope, then Lord Advocate of Scotland, was instructed to bring this bill into Parliament, and in his luminous speech in the House of Commons the learned gentleman, to show the necessity of such regulations, related a most pathetic story of an emigrant vessel arriving in a harbour in one of the British colonies of North America, the whole of the passengers and almost the whole of the crew of which were found dead in their berths, and the few survivors of the crew not able to cast anchor. He also asserted that emigrants who had been some time in the colonies were desirous to get back to their native country, and when they could not accomplish their wishes, were desirous to prevent their friends at home from emigrating, but dared not acquaint them of their now miserable condition but by stratagem, desiring them to consult their Uncle Sandy, and if he advised them to come, then they might proceed. Now, it was well known that Uncle Sandy was dead many years previous. These and many other such like pitiable and affecting passages of the Lord Advocate's speech in the House of Commons blazed through the public prints in Scotland, and were believed, or it was pretended that they were believed, like Gospel, by the Highland lairds and their friends.

" The moment that this bill passed into law, an embargo was laid on all emigrant vessels in British harbours, and this though many of them had already nearly received their complement of passengers, and the whole of the emigrants of the season, after selling their effects, had arrived or were on their way to the seaports to embark. Fortunately, however, for the soldiers of the disbanded Glengarry Fencibles, the greater part of them had got away before the bill came into operation. The Chaplain, having been detained in London on business, after the sailing of his adherents, received a call from the Earl of Selkirk, who proposed to him to join in his plan of taking emigrants to North America. The Chaplain requested his lordship to explain his views and intentions, upon which the Earl stated that he intended to settle those regions between Lakes Huron and Superior with Scotch High-landers, where the climate was nearly similar to that of the north of Scotland, and the soil of a superior quality ; besides, they would enjoy the benefit of the fish with which the lakes teemed, particularly the white fish of the Sault Ste. Marie.

" The Chaplain at first declined this offer on the plea that private business would detain him in London. The Earl then offered him an order for £2,000 upon his agent, as an indemnification for any loss or inconvenience he might experience by so sudden a departure. The Chaplain was a second time compelled to give a refusal and to decline this generous offer of the Earl, declaring at the same time that he felt most grateful for such generosity, but that he could never think of putting himself under so great an obligation to any man ; that the situation which his lordship had selected for his settlement was beyond the jurisdiction of the Government of Upper Canada, and so far from any other location that he was apprehensive that emigrants settling themselves in so remote a region would meet with insuperable difficulties ; that he could by no means induce those with whose interests he was connected to go beyond the protection of the Provincial Government, and, besides, such a settlement would entirely destroy the Northwest Company, as it would cut off the communication between the winterers and Canada ; and as several of the principal members of that Company were his particular friends, no consideration would induce him to enter upon an enterprise that would injure their interest.

" The Chaplain then asked the Earl what could induce a man of his high rank and great fortune, possessing the esteem and confidence of His Majesty's Government and of every public man in Britain, to embark in an enterprise so romantic as that he had just explained. To this the Earl replied that the situation of Great Britain, and indeed of all Europe, was at that moment (September 1803) so very critical and eventful that a man would like to have a more solid footing to stand upon than Europe could offer."

ARRIVAL OF THE CHAPLAIN IN CANADA.

After having settled his affairs, the Chaplain embarked for America and arrived at York, U.C., on the 1st of November, 1804.

And now it is as a Canadian, a BRITISH-Canadian always, that we have to do with him, who, though long since dead, still lives, and ever will continue to dwell in the hearts of his countrymen of Scottish descent.

The Chevalier Macdonell has been good enough to extend to me in the most kind manner the privilege of using such facts as are in his " Reminiscences of the late Honourable and Right Reverend Alexander Macdonell " as would be of service to me in a short sketch of the Bishop's life and works in Canada. Mr. Macdonell reviews his career principally as a Churchman, but it will be my endeavour chiefly to show how it was not only the spiritual welfare, but the worldly prosperity of his people as well he had always in view, and how, though the chief bulwark of the Catholic Church in this Province, indeed one may almost say its founder, he was none the less a true subject of the British Crown, second to no man in his unswerving loyalty to the person and throne of his Sovereign, and how, owing to his extraordinary energy, his ability, the intimate knowledge of the country he acquired during his visits to its different parts, from Quebec to Sarnia, and the great hold he possessed over the Scotch Catholics, who up to and including the war of 1812 were by far the greater portion of his flock, he was able to render that Sovereign service of the highest order when the Americans declared war against Great Britain in 1812, and Canada became the battle ground, as well as on other occasions. But even those of another faith to that to which he clung will not take it amiss, I. am sure, if, incidentally, I refer from time to time to his connection with it. His sentiments regarding those who differed with him in religious matters I am enabled to give in his own words. It would be well if throughout the Province there were more of such tolerance and charity for each other's conscientious views in regard to forms of religions now, though in this county we can boast that the Bishop's words still hold good.

In an address written by him in 1836, he stated :—

" I address my Protestant as well as my Catholic friends because I feel assured that during the long period of four-and-forty years that my intercourse with some of you, and two-and-thirty years with others, has subsisted, no man will say that in promoting your temporal interest I ever made any difference between Catholic and Protestant ; and indeed it would be both unjust and ungrateful in me if I did, for I have found Protestants upon all occasions as ready to meet my wishes and second my efforts to promote the public good as the Catholics themselves : and it is with no small gratification that I here acknowledge having received from Orangemen unequivocal and substantial proofs of disinterested friendship and generosity of heart.

" When a Prime Minister of England (Lord Sidmouth) in 1802 expressed to me his reluctance to permit Scots Highlanders to emigrate to the Canadas from his apprehension that the hold the parent state had of the Canadas was too slender to be permanent, I took the liberty of assuring him that the most effectual way to render that hold strong and permanent was to encourage and facilitate the emigration of Scots Highlanders and Irish Catholics into these colonies. " To the credit and honour of Scots Highlanders be it told that the difference of religion was never known to weaken the bond of friendship ; and Catholic and Protestant have always stood shoulder to shoulder nobly supporting one another during the fiercest tug of battle.

" The loyal and martial character of Highlanders is proverbial. The splendid achievements of your ancestors under a Montrose and a Dundee in support of a fallen Family proved their unshaken adherence to honour and principle, acquired for them the admiration of their opponents, and secured for you, their posterity, the confidence of a liberal and discerning government. You have indeed reason to be proud of such ancestors, and your friends have reason to be proud of your conduct since the first of you crossed the Atlantic."

Efforts on Behalf of His Countrymen.

After his arrival in York, now Toronto, Mr. Macdonell presented his credentials to Lieutenant-General Hunter, then Lieutenant-Governor of the Province, and obtained the land stipulated for his friends according to the order of the Sign Manual. He was immediately appointed to the Mission of St. Raphaels in Glengarry, which remained his headquarters for some twenty-five years. " I had not," he writes in an address, " been long in this Province when I found that few or none of even those of you who were longest settled in the country had legal tenures of your properties. Aware that if trouble or confusion took place in the Province your properties would become uncertain and precarious, and under this impression I proceeded to the seat of Government, where, after some months' hard and unremitting labour through the public offices, I procured for the inhabitants of the Counties of Glengarry and Stormont patent deeds for one hundred and twenty-six thousand acres of land."

That may be taken as a fair indication of the magnitude upon which he was able to conduct affairs, of the extent of his business capacity, and of the influence he always possessed with the Colonial as well as with the Home Government. Another example of his exertions on behalf of the temporal welfare of the people of Glengarry is given in the same address, which was published by him in a time of great public excitement, when he felt called upon to warn the people of the counties against those whom he designated as " wicked, hypocritical radicals, who are endeavouring to drive the Province into rebellion, and cut off every connection between Canada and Great Britain, your Mother Country, and subject you to the domination of Yankee rulers and Lynch law " :—

" I cannot pass over in silence one opportunity I gave you of acquiring property which would have put a large proportion of you at ease for many years—I mean the transport of war-like stores from Lower Canada to the forts and military posts of this Province, which the Governor-in-Chief, Sir George Prevost, and the Quartermaster-General, Sir Sidney Beckwith, offered you at my request.

"After you refused that offer it was given to two gentlemen who cleared from thirty to forty thousand pounds by the bargain."

One of Mr. Macdonell's first and chief objects was the building of churches and establishing of schools, for which purpose he subsequently obtained grants of money from the Home Government, but these grants were not permanent. On his arrival in Upper Canada he found only three Catholic churches in the whole Province, two of wood and one of stone, and only two clergymen—one a Frenchman, utterly ignorant of the English language; the other an Irishman, who left the country soon afterwards.

For more than thirty years Mr. Macdonell's life was devoted to the missions of Upper Canada. He himself, in a letter to Sir Francis Bond Head, referring to an address in the House of Assembly in 1836, in which his character had been aspersed and his motives assailed, gave a statement of the hardships he was called upon to endure in the discharge of his sacred functions when he first came to the country, and of his efforts on behalf of religion subsequently :—

"   *   *   *   Upon entering upon my pastoral duties,

I had the whole of the Province in charge, and without any assist-ance for the space of ten years. During that period I had to travel over the country from Lake Superior to the Province line of Lower Canada, carrying the sacred vestments sometimes on horseback, sometimes on my back, and sometimes in Indian birch canoes, living with savages—without any other shelter or comfort but what their fires and their fares and the branches of the trees afforded ; crossing the great lakes and rivers, and even descending the rapids of the St. Lawrence in their dangerous and wretched craft. Nor were the hardships and privations which I endured among the new settlers and emigrants less than those I had to encounter among the savages themselves, in their miserable shanties, exposed on all sides to the weather and destitute of every comfort. In this way I have been spending my time and my health year after year since I have been in Upper Canada, and not clinging to a seat in the Legislative Coun-cil and devoting my time to political strife, as my accusers are pleased to assert. The erection of five-and-thirty churches and chapels, great and small, although many of them are in an unfinished state, built by my exertion, and the zealous services of two-and-twenty clergymen, the major part of whom have been educated at my own expense, afford a substantial proof that I have not neglected my spiritual functions, nor the care of the souls under my charge ; and if that be not sufficient, I can produce satisfactory documents to prove that I have expended, since I have been in this Province, no less than thirteen thousand pounds of my own private means, besides what I received from other quarters, in building churches, chapels, presbyteries and school houses, in rearing young men for the Church and in promoting general education."

By his zeal, prudence and perseverance, the settlers belonging to his faith, as they multiplied around him, were placed in that sphere and social position to which they were justly entitled.

THE CHAPLAIN SUGGESTS THE FORMATION OF A REGIMENT IN GLENGARRY IN CANADA.

Not long after his arrival in Canada, we find him, in 1807, co-operating with Colonel John Macdonell (Aberchalder),* then Lieu-tenant of the County of Glengarry, in urging on the British Govern-ment through Colonel, afterwards Major-General Sir Isaac Brock, the advisability of raising in Glengarry a Fencible regiment on the ground that a corps of that nature would greatly facilitate any future

* Colonel John Macdonell was the eldest son of Captain Alexander Macdonell, of the King's Royal Regiment of New York, one of the most distinguished Regiments of the Revolutionary War, of which Sir John Johnston, Knight and Baronet, was Colonel-Commandant. Colonel John Macdonell served during the Revolu-tionary War first in the 84th or Royal Highland Emigrant Regiment, and afterwards in command of a company of Butler's Rangers. Colonel Mathews, who had long been on the staff of Sir Frederick Haldimand and Sir Guy Carleton (Lord Dorchester), bore testimony to the fact that he was an active and distinguished partizan of the Royalist cause, stating of himself and his family and clansmen.: " I was at that time quartered at Niagara, and an eye-witness of the gallant and successful exertions of the Macdonells and their depend-ants, by which, in a great measure the upper country of Canada was preserved, for on this little body a fine battalion was soon formed, and afterwards a second." (Letter to the Under Secretary of State for War, 23rd June, 1804.) He was one of the two first members for the County of Glengarry and Speaker of the first House of Assembly of Upper Canada in 1792. He raised in 1796 and com-manded the 2nd Battalion Royal Canadian Volunteer Regiment of Foot, which garrisoned this Province until disbanded with all other Fencible Regiments in the service during the Peace of Amiens in 1802. His brother, Hugh Macdonell, who with him first represented Glengarry, and had previously been an officer in the King's Royal Regiment of New York, was afterwards British Consul-General at Algiers; and another brother, Chichester, who had also been an officer in Butler's Rangers during the Revolutionary War, continued in the service, fought under Sir John Moore at Corunna, for which battle he was awarded a gold medal, and died in India in command of the 34th Regiment of Foot.

project of raising troops for a more general and extended service, besides being a great protection to the Province.

The following correspondence took place :—

"GLENGARRY, January 28th, 1807.

" SIR,—I have the honour to enclose you the proposals for raising a corps of Highland Fencibles in this County, which were submitted to your perusal. The alterations you made are adopted with very few exceptions : should they meet with your approbation, you will be pleased to forward them to the War Office.

" The permanent pay asked for the Field Officers and Chaplain may be considered unusual, but in this instance it is necessary and expedient for carrying the proposals into effect. The Field Officers must undergo a vast deal of trouble, and their time will be as much occupied as if the corps were constantly embodied.

"The County is almost entirely inhabited by Highlanders and their descendants, naturally brave and loyal as subjects, and firmly attached to the British Constitution and Government, yet from their situation and circumstances, being in general possessed of some landed property, and the high run of wages in the county, they are reluctant to quit these advantages to become soldiers. Nothing but a scheme of this nature, headed by gentlemen whom they know and respect, would induce them on any consideration to put themselves under the restraints of military discipline. The Chaplain having served in that capacity in the late Glengarry Fencibles in Great Britain, Ireland and Guernsey, has a claim to the favour of Government. He conducted a number of these people to this country, and having rendered himself useful in many respects to the people at large, has gained so far their confidence that his services in urging and forwarding this matter will be very essential. The adoption and successful issue of the present plan will greatly facilitate any future project of raising troops for a more general and extended nature of service.

" I have the honour to be, Sir,

" Your most obedient, humble servant,

" J. MACDONELL,

" Lieutenant of the County of Glengarry.

" Colonel Brock, &c."

Colonel Brock forwarded Colonel Macdonell's proposal to the War Office, with the following letter to the Right Honourable William Wyndham, then Secretary for War :—

"QUEBEC, February 12, 1807.

" I have the honour to transmit for your consideration a proposal from Lieutenant-Colonel John Macdonell, late of the Royal Canadian Volunteers, for raising a corps among the Scotch settlers in the County of Glengarry, Upper Canada.

" When it is considered that both the Canadas furnish only 200 militia, who are trained to arms, the advantages to be derived from such an establishment must appear very evident.

" The militia force in this country is very small, and were it possible to collect it in time to oppose any serious attempt upon Quebec, the only tenable post, the number would of itself be insufficient to ensure a vigorous defence.

" This corps, being stationed on the confines of the Lower Province, would be always immediately and essentially useful in checking any seditious disposition, which the wavering sentiments of a large population in the Montreal district might at any time manifest. In the event of invasion or other emergency, this force could be easily and expeditiously transported by water to Quebec.

" The extent of the country which these settlers occupy would make the permanent establishment of the staff, and one surgeon in each company, very advisable. I shall not presume to say how far the claims of the field officers to the same indulgence are reasonable and expedient.

" In regard to the Reverend Alexander Macdonell, I beg leave to observe that the men, being all Catholics, it may be deemed a prudent measure to appoint him Chaplain. His zeal and attachment to Government were strongly evinced while filling the office of Chaplain to the Glengarry Fencibles during the rebellion in Ireland, and were graciously acknowledged by His Royal Highness the Commander-in-Chief.

" His influence over the men is deservedly great, and I have every reason to believe that the corps, by his exertions, would be soon completed, and hereafter become a nursery, from which the army might draw a number of hardy recruits.

> " I have, &c.,
>
> " ISAAC BROCK."

Colonel Macdonell's wise suggestion was not at the time carried into effect, but a few years afterwards, when our relations with the United States had arrived at a crisis, the British Government adopted his plan, and gladly availed itself of the services of the hardy band of Highland loyalists, who had made their home in Glengarry in Canada, and, fortunately, though Colonel John Macdonell was unable to aid his Sovereign and his country, the patriotic Chaplain, with the assistance, as will be seen, of another namesake and clansman, raised and organized the Glengarry Light Infantry Regiment, which fought through the War of 1812, and caused the name of Glengarry to be respected by those who gloried in the freedom of British institutions, and feared by those who sought to overthrow them.

At this time there was but one Catholic Bishop in the whole of the British dominions in North America ; the entire country from the Atlantic to the Pacific coast formed one diocese under the jurisdiction of the Bishop of Quebec.   In 1806, Monseigneur Plessis, the eleventh Bishop of Quebec, succeeded to that See on the death of Bishop Denant.   One of his first thoughts was to divide his immense diocese.   In announcing the death of his predecessor, Monseigneur Plessis expressed a hope that the Court of Rome would soon come to an understanding with the Court of St. James for the erection of a Metropolitan and some Bishoprics in British North America. Meantime, he petitioned the Holy See to allow him three coadjutors, one in Montreal, one in Upper Canada and a third in Nova Scotia. his intention being to recommend as coadjutor for Upper Canada Mr. Macdonell, who had already been placed among the number of his Vicars-General.   Local difficulties, however, added to the disturbed state of Europe and the war which occurred between Great Britain and the United States, delayed the consummation of the project Monseigneur Plessis had in view for several years.

When war broke out in 1812, Mr. Macdonell (Maighster Alastair as he was then known among the Highlanders) could, owing to the nature of his sacred profession, scarcely be said to have been in his element, but when there was fighting to be done, "the Chaplain" wanted to be close at hand to see that it was well done. It was a favourite saying of his that "every man of his name should be either a priest or a soldier," and had he not been a priest he would have been a great soldier. He had all the qualities of one. His stature was immense and his frame herculean. He stood six feet four, and was stout in proportion; he had undaunted courage, calm, cool judgment, resolute will and a temper almost imperturbable; he had the endurance of his race, fatigue and privation were as nothing to him; he was a man of great natural ability, great parts and a great personality which impressed all brought in contact with him; he inspired confidence, admiration and respect, but above all he was a born leader of men. The gain to the Church was great, the loss to the army correspondingly great when he was ordained at Valadolid !

It was necessary at once to raise soldiers for the emergency. It was "the Chaplain" who fired the heather ! He had previously raised a regiment. He now raised another for his Sovereign. He was an unerring judge of men, and he nominated for his colleague the man best fitted for the task, and Captain George Macdonell was commissioned by the Commander-in-Chief to co-operate with him, and this gallant officer of the King's Regiment and "the Chaplain" had the Glengarry Light Infantry, who numbered four hundred rank and file, in the field by the 1st of May, "and we find that on Sir George Prevost's issuing orders to recruit for a still higher establishment, the officers engaged to double the number and did it." *

The Glengarry Light Infantry Regiment thus raised was placed on the regular establishment of the British army, and served in the most conspicuous and creditable manner throughout the War of 1812-14, taking part in no less than fourteen general engagements. They were present, amongst others, at the taking of Ogdensburg, Fort Covington and Oswego; at the attack on Sackett's Harbour, and at the battle at York. They lost three companies with their officers at the landing of the Americans at Fort George, and were also at

* Auchinleck.

the battles of Stoney Creek and Lundy's Lane. The officers of the first battalion were as follows :—

GLENGARRY LIGHT INFANTRY FENCIBLE REGIMENT.

Colonel—Edward Baynes.
Lieutenant-Colonel—Francis Battersby.
Major—George Macdonell.

Captains.

Andrew Liddell,	Robert Macdouall,
John Jenkins,	Thomas Fitzgerald,
R. M. Cochrane,	Foster Weeks,
D. Macpherson,	W. Roxborough.

Lieutenants.

A. McMillan,	Walter Kerr.
James Stewart,	Aneas Shaw,
Anthony Leslie,	William Kemble,
H. S. Hughes,	James B. Macaulay.

Ensigns.

Roderick Matheson,	James Mackay,
Angus Macdonell,	Byland Smith,
James Robins,	Joseph Frobisher,
William Maclean,	Alexander Macdonell.

Pay-master—Anthony Leslie.
Adjutant—John Mackay.
Quarter-master—John Watson.
Agents—Greenwood, Cox and Company.

The Chaplain and Captain Macdonell not only filled up the ranks of the Regiment in Glengarry, but distributed rather more commissions among the gentlemen of the County than was anticipated by or altogether pleasing to the officers at headquarters, as appears from the following letter :—

MAJOR-GENERAL BROCK TO COLONEL BAYNES.

" YORK, January 26, 1812.

" Capt. Macdonell, accompanied by the priest, arrived here some days ago. The badness of the weather has prevented his return as soon as he first proposed. All the junior commissions being already disposed of among the youths of Glengarry, I fear that little will be done in this part of the Province towards recruiting the intended corps. A few idlers may be picked up; but, without the aid of persons of influence, no great number can be expected, unless indeed the militia be called out, and land promised.

"Understanding from Captain Macdonell that the Commander of the forces had applied to the Prince Regent for permission to offer some of the waste land of the Crown as an inducement to the Scotch emigrants to enlist, I stated the circumstances to Council, and have much pleasure in assuring His Excellency, that should he be of opinion the present aspect of affairs calls for prompt measures, and that a direct promise of land would accelerate the recruiting, this Government will readily pledge itself to grant one, or even two, hundred acres to such as enlist on the terms proposed by His Excellency. This will be deviating largely from the King's instructions; but in these eventful and critical times, the Council conceives that an expression from His Excellency of the necessity of the measure will be sufficient to warrant a departure from the usual rules. Should His Excellency think it expedient to act immediately, and authorize a direct offer of land, I have no doubt that a number of young men might be collected between Kingston and Amherstburg, in which case His Excellency may sanction the raising of two additional companies under my superintendence.

"I have, &c.,

"ISAAC BROCK."

"The Bishop," as Colonel Coffin styles him, though he was but a priest at the time, "had been most active in raising and recruiting the Glengarries during the preceding winter. The fiery cross had passed through the land and every clansman had obeyed the summons." * Well was he in a position to state in after years, "The Second Glengarry Regiment, raised in the Province when the Government of the United States of America invaded and expected to make a conquest of Canada, was planned by me and partly raised by my influence. My zeal in the service of my country and my exertions in the defence of this Province were acknowledged

---

* Coffin, page 92.

by His late Majesty through Lord Bathurst, then Secretary of State for the Colonies. My salary was then increased and a seat was assigned to me in the Legislative Council as a distinguished mark of my Sovereign's favour; an honour," he continues, striking out at some who had the hardihood to traduce him, "I should consider it a disgrace to resign, although I can hardly ever expect to sit in Council, nor do I believe that Lord Glenelg who knows something of me would expect that I should show so much imbecility in my latter days as to relinquish a mark of honour conferred upon me by my Sovereign to gratify the vindictive malice of a few unprincipled radicals."

But his attention was not confined to Glengarry alone, nor his vast energy to the raising of men; now he was to be found at York, again at Quebec, in communication with General Brock, Sir George Prevost and other leading military men, suggesting plans of various kinds, which readily met with acceptance, urging that the waste lands of the Crown should be offered to emigrants to encourage them to enlist, and with the eye of an old campaigner, seeing that communication was kept open between Quebec and the Upper Country of Canada.

MAJOR GENERAL BROCK TO SIR GEORGE PREVOST.

"YORK, January 26, 1812.

"The very serious inconvenience which the inhabitants of this Province experience for want of a sufficient land communication with Lower Canada induces me to trouble you on the subject. The Reverend Mr. Macdonell, of Glengarry, the bearer of this letter, is so well qualified to explain the causes which have hitherto impeded the cutting of a road to connect the two Provinces that I need not detain Your Excellency, particularly as reference can be had to Lieutenant-Colonel Bruyeres, who, having been employed by Sir James Craig to ascertain the grounds upon which a difficulty arose in the attainment of so desirable an object, can give every necessary information," and I find that a measure having been adopted to this end in the following year (15th February, 1813), the Reverend Alexander Macdonell, Alexander McMillan, Esquire, and Allan Macdonell, Esquire, were appointed commissioners to open a road between Upper and Lower Canada under the Act 53, George III., Chapter 4. I presume that the road then built is that now known as " the King's Road."

When Ogdensburg was taken by the Glengarry Fencibles and the Glengarry Militia under Colonel George Macdonell * on 23rd February, 1813, the Chaplain was with his clansmen. A good story of him is told me by my friend, Mr. Kenneth Ross, of Lancaster, whose father was wounded in the attack. Ross was carried into the house of an inn-keeper near Prescott, a half-Yankee, like many of his ilk along the border. The Chaplain saw that the wounded man was as much in need of stimulants as of priestly counsel, and went at once in search of some brandy. Excuses of various kinds were made by the woman of the house. Her husband was absent and had the keys, and so on. The Chaplain told her he would take no denial, and that if she did not procure the brandy forthwith he would have it in short order. She still demurred, whereupon he walked to the tap-room door, and with one kick lifted it off its hinges, and not only Mr. Ross, but all others of His Majesty's liege subjects had all the brandy they required after their hard day's fighting. Though Mr. Ross was a Presbyterian and the Chaplain a Catholic Priest, I doubt if he could have been better served in his extremity even by a Minister of his own denomination.

---

* Colonel George Macdonell was awarded one of the two gold medals given for the Battle of Chateauguay, and was created a Companion of the Bath. He afterwards commanded the 79th Regiment of Foot.

Again Visits England—Is Appointed Bishop of Upper Canada—A Coadjutor Nominated.

In 1816, Mr. Macdonell returned to England and waited upon Mr. Addington, then Viscount Sidmouth, who introduced him to Earl Bathurst, then principal Secretary of State for the Colonies. Part of his mission was to induce the Home Government to favour the measure proposed by the Bishop of Quebec for the division of that Diocese, in which undertaking he succeeded to a certain extent.

In July, 1817, the See of Rome separated Nova Scotia from the Diocese of Quebec, and created that Province into an Apostolic-Vicariate. At the same time, Lord Castlereagh induced the Court of Rome to erect two other Apostolic-Vicariates, one formed of Upper Canada, and the other of New Brunswick, Prince Edward Island and the Magdalen Islands. Mr. Macdonell returned to Canada in 1817. On the 12th January, 1819, he was nominated Bishop of Resina, i.p.i., and Vicar-Apostolic of Upper Canada, and was consecrated on the 31st December, 1820, in the Church of the Ursuline Convent, Quebec.

In 1825, Bishop Macdonell returned to England for two principal objects: to obtain assistance in his laborious duties and to induce the Home Government to withdraw its opposition to the appointment of titular Bishops in Canada. On the same occasion he visited Rome. He succeeded in both instances, and returned to Canada in 1826. In the same year the Reverend W. P. Macdonald, for twenty years Vicar-General, and well-known throughout the Province, came to Canada to take charge of the Bishop's intended Seminary for ecclesiastics at St. Raphael's. Mr. Macdonald was born at Eberlow, Banffshire, Scotland, on the 25th March, 1771. He was sent at an early age by Bishop Hay to the College of Douay, which he was compelled to leave on the outbreak of the French Revolution. His studies were finished at the Scots' College at

Valladolid. He was ordained there on the 29th November, 1790, and returned at once to Scotland, where for twelve years he discharged the laborious and humble duties of a Missionary Priest. About the year 1801, the British Cabinet, having formed the project of conveying Ferdinand VII. from Bayonne, Mr. Macdonald was recommended as a fit person to be employed in that enterprise, particularly as he had perfect mastery of the French and Spanish languages. He accordingly proceeded on his mission, and cruised off Quiberon for some time ; but in consequence of some information received by the French Directory, the project of the British Government was abandoned. Mr. Macdonald was afterwards employed on the British Embassy in Spain for four years, after which he was appointed a Chaplain in the regular army. He was a thorough scholar and a polished gentleman. In 1830 he published the "Catholic" newspaper at Kingston and resumed it at Hamilton from 1841 to 1844. Universally regretted, he died at St. Michael's Palace, Toronto, on Good Friday, April 2nd, 1847, and was buried in the Cathedral on the Gospel side of the choir.

The Seminary at St. Raphael's (College of Iona) was a very modest affair, but it had the honour to produce some of the most efficient missionaries of the time, among whom may be mentioned the Reverend George Hay, of St. Andrews, the Reverend Michael Brennan, of Belleville, and the Reverend Edward Gordon, of Hamilton. Nature had furnished Mr. Hay with an extra little finger on each hand, which were amputated prior to his ordination. While at the Montreal Seminary, one of the professors is reported to have said of him, " He is a good boy, but he will never sing Mass." Singing was, in fact, a rare accomplishment among the early Scottish and Irish missionaries. The Bishop himself always said Low Mass and never attempted to sing, not even the ordinary Episcopal benediction at the end. " I once took lessons," he said, " for six months, but after my teacher got his money he discovered I had no voice."

Upper Canada was erected into a Bishopric by Leo XII. on the 14th of February, 1826, and Bishop Macdonell appointed first Bishop under the title of Regiopolis, or Kingston. His diocese comprised the present Province of Ontario, and has since been subdivided into the Dioceses of Kingston, Toronto, Hamilton, London, Ottawa, Pembroke, Peterborough and Alexandria. *

Advancing age and increased responsibility forced the Bishop to apply for a coadjutor, and Mr. Weld, of Lulworth Castle, a descendant and representative of one of the oldest Catholic families of England, who, on the death of his wife—like another eminent Cardinal of the present day—had taken orders, was selected and consecrated Bishop of Amycla and Coadjutor of Upper Canada, on the 6th of August, 1826. By the advice of his friends and medical advisers, Bishop Weld remained some years in England and afterwards went to Rome, where, in March, 1830, he was nominated Cardinal by Pius VIII.

The Presbytery (abandoned in 1889 on the erection of the one built on the west side of the Church) and the present Church at St. Raphael's were built in anticipation of the arrival of Bishop Weld, but although always fully intending to go to Canada, he closed his days at Rome on the 10th of April, 1837. His funeral discourse was pronounced by Doctor (afterwards Cardinal) Wiseman, Rector of the English College at Rome. Bishop Macdonell obtained many favours from Rome through the influence of his intended coadjutor.

After Bishop Macdonell's last return from England, he resided for some years at York, in the house still standing on the south-east corner of Jarvis (then Nelson) and Duchess streets. The Bishop went to Kingston about the year 1836, and resided there during the remainder of his stay in Canada. The Chevalier W. J. Macdonell, whose ipsissima verba I have by permission, in many instances, adopted, states :—

" The Bishop was a thorough Highlander, and did not relish remarks that seemed to reflect on the manners and customs of his countrymen. The writer one day gave his unasked opinion that oatmeal was not wholesome, inasmuch as he had known several young fellows brought upon on that diet whose skins were very rough. The Bishop replied rather curtly, ' You don't know what you are talking about.' On another occasion the writer was reading from

* Alexandria is named after Bishop Macdonell. It was he who built the mill there, which was the beginning of the town.

Bercastel's 'History of the Church,' an account of the hardships undergone by the missionaries sent by St. Vincent de Paul to keep alive the faith in the Highlands and Islands of Scotland. The historian states that the missionaries frequently passed several days without food, and at the end of that time their only refection was oatmeal cakes or barley bread, with cheese or salt butter. 'Under the circumstances,' remarked the Bishop, 'I think they fared very well.' Although the Bishop 'had no voice,' he was fond of the national music. A great dinner was given at the old British American Hotel, in Kingston, to Sir James Macdonell, 'the hero of Hougoumont.' The whole town attended. The Bishop was Chairman. A regimental piper in the garb of old Gaul, with his pibroch in full blast, marched round the table. Vicar-General Macdonell, who, though every inch a Scotchman, was a bit of a wag, declared that every time the piper passed behind the Bishop the latter inclined his head to one side that his ears might be tickled by the ribbons and tassels of the passing pipers!"

THE BISHOP'S JUBILEE.

Ordained Priest at Valladolid on the 16th of February, 1787, Bishop Macdonell kept his jubilee on the 16th of February, 1837. The following account is taken from the papers of the time :—

"A novel and interesting ceremony took place to-day in the Parish Church of St. Raphael, Glengarry, which drew a crowd of more than 2,000 persons into that spacious edifice. It is a custom of great antiquity in the Catholic Church for a clergyman on completing his fiftieth year of priesthood to celebrate a jubilee of thanksgiving to God and renew his vows to continue in the faithful discharge of his pastoral duties for the remaining years of his life. Bishop Macdonell having on this day completed the fiftieth year of his priesthood, came down from Kingston for the purpose of complying with this ancient ordinance of his Church. The Superior and gentlemen of the Seminary of Montreal expressed an earnest desire that the ceremony should be performed in the magnificent Parish Church of that city ; but the Bishop found it more in accordance with his own feelings, as he knew it would be more gratifying to his countrymen and former flock, among whom he had spent upwards of thirty years in the discharge of the duties of an apostolic missionary, to appear before them on this occasion, which would probably be the last in his life. The Bishop of Montreal and many of the clergy of Lower Canada who wished to be present were prevented by the depth of snow and the severity of the weather. Nineteen priests, however, attended, and all the Protestant and Catholic gentlemen of the county, besides several from the County of Stormont and the Ottawa district. Many of these latter gentlemen were also Protestants, but their long acquaintance and high respect for Bishop Macdonell induced them to travel more than fifty miles across the country in the most severe snowstorm that has been known for many years. The Bishop addressed his countrymen before Mass in Gaelic, their native tongue ; he called to their recollection the destitute state in which he found their mission, and indeed the whole Province, in regard to religion on his arrival in the country in 1804, there being no clergy, no churches, no presbyteries, nor schools ; and what ren- dered the labour of a missionary more arduous, no roads. His pastoral labours were not confined to the County of Glengarry ; they extended from one end of the Province to the other, and for many years he had no fellow-labourer to assist him within a distance of seven hundred miles. Under such overwhelming difficulties, he had much reason to acknowledge and thank the merciful Providence of Almighty God for making him, although unworthy, the humble instru- ment of procuring for them the many temporal and spiritual advant- ages which they at present enjoy. He trusted that they would pay proper respect and submission to his worthy coadjutor, the Bishop of Tabracca, whose ardent zeal to promote the glory of God and the interests of the Catholic religion had induced him to leave a quiet and comfortable position, where he was respected and beloved among his own countrymen, to encounter privations, fatigues and difficulties in this Province. In conclusion, as this might be the last oppor- tunity he should have of appearing before them in this world, Bishop Macdonell begged their forgiveness for any bad example he had

given them, and for any neglect or omission of his duty during his
ministry among them for so many years; trusting much to their
prayers and supplications to the Throne of Mercy on his behalf, to
enable him to prepare his long and fearful accounts against the great
and awful day of reckoning, which, in the course of nature, could
not be far distant: and he promised them that he would never cease
to offer up his unworthy prayers for their spiritual and temporal welfare. Tears flowed in abundance from the eyes of the Bishop and
his hearers during this short but affecting discourse. After Mass,
Vicar-General Macdonald delivered an eloquent and impressive
sermon, and the ceremony being finished, the clergy and many of the
gentlemen repaired to the presbytery, where all the clergy and such
of the gentlemen as could be prevailed upon to remain had a comfortable dinner prepared for them by the coadjutor."

The Bishop Anticipates the Coming Rebellion and Warns His Flock.

In 1836, Bishop Macdonell foresaw the coming storm, and in an
address to the Catholic and Protestant freeholders of the Counties of
Glengarry and Stormont, from which I have previously quoted,
exhorted them at the elections then imminent faithfully to discharge
their duty to their Sovereign and their country by electing men of
sound and loyal principles. There was no mistaking where the
Bishop stood. He left no room for doubt as to that:—

" Your gracious and benevolent Sovereign sent you out as his
representative a personage distinguished for abilities, knowledge and
integrity, to redress all the grievances and abuses that had crept
into the Government of this Province since its first establishment;
but instead of meeting him with cordiality, and offering their co-
operation in the important work of reform, what do the radicals do?
Why, they assail him, like hell-hounds, with every possible abuse,
indignity and insult, and would feign make you believe that they are
your friends and the friends of the country, although implacable
enemies of yourselves, your religion and your country: and this

they proved by stopping the money which the Government had been
giving for some years past towards building and repairing Catholic
churches, supporting Catholic schools and maintaining Catholic
clergy.

"It has been with Government money that the Catholics of
Glengarry have been able to proceed with the Parish Church of St.
Raphael's, after allowing it to remain in a state of decay for the space
of sixteen or seventeen years, from the inability of the parishioners to
finish it ; and it has been by the aid of Government money that
almost every other Catholic church in the Province has been brought
to the state it is now in—and further advances were ready to be
made towards completing them, when, by the false representations
of the Radicals, orders came from home to stop the issuing of the
money, and the consequence is that the greater part of those churches
are left in an unfinished and insecure state.

"At the same time that those Radicals who aim at the destruc-
tion of our Holy Religion are loud in their complaints against Government for affording me assistance towards establishing it on a permanent foundation in this Province, they are cutting and carving lucrative
situations for themselves, and filling their own pockets and those of
their champion O'Grady " (an abandoned Priest whom the Bishop
was obliged to excommunicate) " with your money and that of your
fellow subjects. It was for this purpose that they stopped the sup-
plies last session and thereby prevented the issue of the money
which was to be laid out on public roads, canals and other improve-
ments of the Province."

1837–8.

It was stated at the time that during the absence of the regulars,
Bishop Macdonell had charge of the garrison at Kingston. The
eastern portion of the Province, however, except on the occasion of
the raid made by banditti from the United States in the neighbour-
hood of Prescott, was not much disturbed during the rebellion. Rebels
did not appear to be indigenous to its soil. Glengarry was able to
spare two regiments to assist in quelling the revolt in Lower Canada,

while two others were on duty elsewhere. Some of the Priests of the Diocese, however, amongst whom was the Bishop's nephew, the late Vicar-General Angus Macdonell, had a painful duty to perform, as many of the American invaders, notably Von Schultz and others who were taken at the Windmill, were sent to Kingston, and such of them as were Catholics, including Von Schultz, had to be prepared for death by them. They were obliged to attend Fort Henry with the Sheriff to select for their ministrations such of the prisoners as were from time to time doomed to the last penalty. Sheriff Macdonell was supposed to have lost his reason from the shocks produced by the trying scenes he was almost daily obliged to witness in the discharge of his duty.

The Bishop Establishes Regiopolis College.

Bishop Macdonell had experienced great difficulty in obtaining properly educated men for the priesthood, which want seriously retarded the improvement of the Catholic population. He was fully aware that the evil could be remedied only by the building and endowment of a Seminary for the education of his clergy. He obtained an Act of Incorporation from the Legislature and appropriated a piece of land for the erection of a suitable building. At a meeting convened by the Bishop at his residence on the 10th October, 1837, it was resolved that the Bishop, his nephew, Vica-General Angus Macdonell, and Dr. Thomas Rolph should proceed to England for the purpose of collecting funds for the erection of a Catholic College in Upper Canada. It was the anxious desire of the Bishop that a Priesthood should be raised in the Province, fearing God, attached to the Institutions of the country, and using their assiduous efforts to maintain its integrity; until such an establishment was founded he could not be responsible for his clergy as he would wish to be. Such was the reason for the foundation of Regiopolis College, but it does not appear to have realized the hopes of its eminent founder, and has for many years past been closed.

FORMATION OF THE HIGHLAND SOCIETY OF CANADA.

Prior to the Bishop's departure for England, a farewell dinner was given him by the Highland Society of Upper Canada at Carmino's Hotel, Kingston.

Such a proceeding was eminently proper, for no man had done more to maintain the honour and dignity of the Highland name in Canada than had the Bishop. I will here quote from a little pamphlet containing "An Account of the Highland Society of Canada," compiled by my father, Archibald John Macdonell (the younger of Greenfield), Secretary and one of the Directors of the Society in 1844, as it shows how deep an interest Bishop Macdonell took in all that concerned the Society of which he was virtually the founder. I will first give the introductory letter. It was addressed to a well known Glengarry man, Mr. Macdonald of Gart, who lived for many years on what was formerly known as the Grey's Creek property in the Township of Charlottenburgh, on the River St. Lawrence.

" To John Macdonald, Esquire, President of the Highland Society of Canada.

" MY DEAR SIR,—When circumstances have forced a people to abandon their native country and seek the means of subsistence among foreigners, or in the Colonies of their own country, they carry with them as a matter of course, the feelings and the prejueices— alike honourable—which they had imbibed at home ; to perpetuate which in the land of their adoption, to instil into the minds of their children the same principles they themselves had been taught, to teach them to love above all others—above even that of their own nativity—the country from which stern necessity alone could have driven their fathers, and with which all their fathers nearest and dearest associations are connected, and to rivet the connection between their new country and their old, among other means emigrants have invariably adopted the formation of national societies. It cannot be otherwise than that these societies must answer the end for which they were instituted, and arguing with the intention of proving it, would be supererogatory and useless.

"With such objects in view did the Highlanders in London establish the Highland Society of London, with what success is well known. That this venerable and distinguished institution has mainly contributed to preserve in its purity the Highland character, and has done more to promote the general welfare of the Highlands, than any other association, is a general and well-grounded opinion.

"While the Highlanders of Canada remember with gratitude that to the late lamented Bishop Macdonell they owe the establishment of a branch of that society among them, they cannot forget that to you they are indebted for its organization after it had ceased operations for fifteen years.

"The generous and patriotic motives that animated you in the work cannot be sufficiently appreciated ; but I am sure that you feel yourself in some measure recompensed for all your trouble and anxiety, when you consider how much the Society has already done to promote the objects for which it was established and re-organized.

"In order that those objects may be more generally and more clearly known and understood, I' have, by permission, compiled an account of the Society, containing the speech of Mr. Simon Mac-Gillivray to the gentlemen who took part in its formation, from which more can be learned of the history and purposes of the Parent Society than from any remarks I could make ; the constitution and by-laws, a list of the members, and such other information the publication of which, I thought, would in any way tend to serve the Society, or interest and gratify its members.

"I do not think it necessary to appeal to the feelings of our countrymen for a liberal support of the institution ; this has already been given, and to their credit be it spoken, that from Quebec to Amherstburg the utmost enthusiasm has been shown in support of this Society, which I hope and believe will be the instrument of preserving in Canada the recollection of the Highland name, and with it the chivalrous and devoted loyalty, and other noble qualities which made the ancient Highland character the first in the world. Should the national character be doomed to give way to the encroachments of modern innovations, you will have, in an eminent degree, the satisfaction of knowing that you made an effort to save it.

"As a member of the Highland Society of Canada, I joined most heartily in the mark of grateful respect shown by it to its venerated founder: and as such I desire to express my gratitude to its preserver, while as a private individual, I shew my respect for the gentleman by inscribing this small compilation to you.

"I am, my dear Sir,
"Very truly yours,
"ARCH. JOHN MACDONELL,
"(Younger of Greenfield.)
"Greenfield, Glengarry, 22nd January, 1844."

THE SECRETARY'S NARRATIVE.

"The Right Reverend Bishop Macdonell, whose whole life was spent in the service of his countrymen, rightly judging that the establishment of such an institution would be of very material benefit to them, solicited and obtained from the Highland Society of London, of which he was a distinguished member, a commission to establish a branch in Canada, of which number the Bishop himself was one. Upon its receipt, the gentlemen to whom it was addressed, being of opinion that the Counties of Glengarry and Stormont, forming the great Highland Settlement in Canada, would offer at once the greatest facility for the establishment, and the most favourable field for the operation of such an association, determined to hold the institutional meeting in them, and accordingly called a meeting of such gentlemen as were willing to aid, at the house of Mr. Angus Macdonell, at St. Raphael's, in Glengarry.

"A highly respectable meeting took place in accordance with the requisition on the 10th November, 1818, over which Mr. Simon MacGillivray, one of the Vice-Presidents of the Highland Society of London, presided, and at which were present among others, three of the best and finest Highland gentlemen this Province ever saw, the late Honourable William MacGillivray, the late Bishop Macdonell and the late Honourable Neil MacLean, all of whom 'though dead still live in the hearts of their countrymen.' The Commission under which the Branch was to be constituted, being produced, was read as follows :—

"' Whereas, the Highland Society of London was instituted in the year 1778 to associate together in the British Metropolis, the nobility landed proprietors and others of the Highlands, together with their descendants, the officers of Highland Corps and gentlemen connected by family alliance with, or who have rendered some signal service to that part of the Kingdom ; for preserving the language, martial spirit dress, music, and antiquities of the ancient Caledonians ; for rescuing from oblivion the valuable remains of Celtic literature ; for the establishment and support of Gaelic ; for relieving distressed High landers at a distance from their native homes, and for promoting the welfare and general improvement of the northern parts of the Island of Great Britain.

"'And whereas,the society to extend the benefit of this Institution and to unite together in a central union their countrymen whereve situated, have resolved to issue Commissions for the establishmen of Branches thereof in the British Colonies and other place at home and abroad, where Highlanders are resident, and being extremely desirous that a Branch should be established in Canada you are hereby empowered and requested, in pursuance of this reso lution, to form a Branch of the Highland Society of London in Canada accordingly, with authority to make such by-laws as may be necessary for the management thereof, in conformity with the principles and rules of the said Society.

(Signed.)   "' FREDERICK.

"' President.

"' To William MacGillivray, Esq.,
    Angus Shaw, Esq.,
    Rev. Alexander Macdonell,
    John Macdonald, Esq.,
    Henry Mackenzie, Esq.'

" The commission being laid on the table, the Chairman, in opening the business of the meeting stated, ' that the best account of the objects and views of the Highland Society was to be found in the Commission just read, and it only remained for him to give some account of the origin and history of the Society, and to offer some suggestions in regard to the best mode of proceeding in the establishment of the proposed branch thereof, by the gentlemen whom he had the honour of addressing.

" ' The Highland Society of London was at first merely a convivial club, established by some young Highlanders, as a place of resort, where they went to spend occasional evenings among their countrymen, and to refer to occurrences, recollections and feelings endeared to them by early associations ; to resume the garb and language of their ancestors, and to introduce the songs of the bards and the music of the minstrels which had always bestowed and distinguished a peculiar character on the social meetings of Highlanders.

" ' Happily, the Highland Club then established soon became known to many public-spirited individuals of distinction and influence in society, and it occurred to them that the design might be extended and applied to public objects of the highest national utility. A meeting of noblemen and gentlemen was accordingly assembled, and the Society was established for the public purposes recited in the Commission—with such views and with the support of a succession of men of the first rank and consideration in the country, it was scarely necessary to add, that the Society had flourished and was now in the highest state of prosperity. It comprised in the list of its members, with few, if any exceptions, all the noblemen and gentlemen connected with the Highlands, and who usually resorted to London.

" ' The names of several of the Princes graced the rolls of the Institution, and the Prince Regent himself had condescended to become a member and to accept the Highland distinction of Chief of the Society. In order further to increase the utility, and to insure the permanency of the Highland Society, it has been incorporated by an act of Parliament, and might therefore be justly described a benevolent, a literary, and an antiquarian Society, with lawful authority superior to any other similar Institution in the United Kingdom.

" ' To enter into any details respecting the beneficient services to
the Highlands, and to the country at large, that are rendered by this
Society, or even to enumerate them, would occupy far too much of
the time of the evening, and therefore he (the Chairman) wished to
suggest on what points it would be expedient for the Society about to
be established in Canada to follow the example of the Parent Society,
and what other objects conducive to the improvement and to the
peculiar interests of this Province might be associated with those
specified in the Commission. The objects of the Highland Society
of London were first for preserving the language, martial spirit, dress,
music and antiquities of the ancient Caledonians, and thus maintaining a bond of association wherever they should meet. This wish
to preserve in the present day the language and customs of other
times might possibly be called prejudice, but so also might many of
the noblest feelings which can actuate the human mind. Modern
latitude of opinion might stigmatize as prejudice the loyalty of the
patriot and the devotedness of the soldier; the self-called citizen of
the world might, in the language of universal philanthrophy, blame
love of country itself, as a narrow and prejudiced feeling, and while
we attempt to measure principles by their utility, might in fact
reduce them to individual and sordid selfishness. But surely to a
meeting of Highlanders it was unnecessary to enlarge on this point,
or to explain how love of country might resolve itself into love of
one's own countrymen, and thence into attachment to the peculiar
customs which distinguished those countrymen, and, even on the
score of utility, to the garb which distinguished the Highland soldier,
of the language in which the deeds of his forefathers were celebrated,
and the music which animated him in the day of battle—all of which
were objects well deserving the attention of those who wished to
preserve unimpaired the martial spirit, and devote themselves to the
service of the Country.

" ' The next object of the Society, viz. : the rescuing from oblivion
the valuable remains of Gaelic literature, was one which he supposed
could not be much promoted in this Province ; but if any such
remains were still extant among any of the more ancient emigrants,
it was needless to point out the propriety of immediate attention to
them.

" ' The object next specified, viz.: the establishment and support of Gaelic schools and the relieving of distressed Highlanders at a distance from their native homes, were both peculiarly applicable to the state of society in this Province, where the means of bestowing generally the benefits of education were still very deficient, and where many Highland emigrants were daily arriving in a state of great poverty and distress.

" 'The object of the Parent Society for promoting the improvement and general welfare of the northern parts of the Island of Great Britain would probably in this branch thereof be modified, so as to apply to the improvement and general welfare of the Highland Settlements in this Province, and though he was deficient in local knowledge on the subject, yet the information he received left no room to doubt, that by a judicious distribution of premiums for agricultural improvement and by other means within the reach of the Society, much might be done towards promoting an object so desirable.

" ' This mention of premiums naturally led him to consider the means of providing them and of contributing to the other objects of the Society, which it was evident, could only be done by subscriptions to be paid by members ; and in fixing the rate of such subscriptions the meeting would have to consider, on the one side, the expediency of raising ample funds to promote such laudable purposes, and on the other, the danger of deterring eligible members from coming forward by exacting too high a contribution on admission into the Society.

" ' On this point, and indeed on many others on which he had touched, he (the Chairman) had derived much information and assistance from a gentleman well-known to the meeting, and highly esteemed by all to whom he was known ; a gentleman active and indefatigable in promotion every object connected with the prosperity of the Province, and to whose individual exertions the meeting was indebted for obtaining the Commission under which they were then ʼassembled, and for organizing the measures to be brought before them.   This gentleman was the Reverend Alexander Macdonell, and he (the Chairman) stated that this gentleman's previous approbation of the propositions to be submitted to the meeting would of itself be sufficient to secure them a favourable reception. It only remained to speak of the internal regulations of the Society.'

"Mr. MacGillivray then proceeded to discuss some matters of internal economy, particularly the date of the general annual meeting of the Society, and after suggesting the anniversary of the Battle of Alexandria (which day, the 21st of March, had been selected by the Parent Society) and the anniversary of the Battle of Bannockburn, urged that the 18th of June should be adopted, as on that day Scotchmen, Englishmen and Irishmen had stood shoulder to shoulder at Waterloo, for the good not only of Britain alone, but of all Europe and even the civilized world, against a far more formidable man than King Edward—a day on which Highlanders had maintained the reputation of their country and emulated the deeds of their ancestors ; and that day was accordingly selected.

"It was then resolved, That it is expedient to establish in this Province a Branch of the Highland Society of London, to be called the Highland Society of Canada.*

"After a constitution, which declared the objects of the newly-formed Society similar to those of the Parent Society, had been adopted, the meeting proceeded to the election of office-bearers, when the Reverend Alexander Macdonell communicated the highly-gratifying intelligence that he had solicited and obtained the consent of His Excellency Sir Peregrine Maitland to become President, and the following gentlemen were unanimously elected to and, with the exception of the President, were immediately installed into their respective offices :—

"President :
"Sir Peregrine Maitland, K.C.B., &c., &c., &c.

"Vice-Presidents :
"The Reverend Alexander Macdonell,
"Colonel the Honourable Neil MacLean,
"Lieutenant-Colonel Donald Greenfield Macdonell.

"Treasurer :
"Alexandria Fraser, Esquire.

---

*See Appendix.

"Secretary :

"Archibald MacLean, Esquire.

"Directors :

"Roderick MacLeod,

"Alexander MacLean,

"Alexander Wilkinson, Esquires.

"After a vote of thanks had been given to the Honourable William MacGillivray and Mr. Simon MacGillivray for their attendance at, and able assistance in, the formation of the Society, the meeting broke up."

My father states that the Society continued in active operations for several years, and contributed largely to the objects for which it was formed, drawing upon itself the blessing of many distressed Highlanders, whom it relieved at a distance from their native home ; several liberal contributions in money were given to assist gentlemen engaged in the publication of works in the Gaelic language, and a succession of premiums to Gaelic scholars, performers on the bagpipes and the best dressed Highlanders ; nor were the remains of Celtic literature neglected, while some collection of Gaelic poetry was made.

Owing, however, to the death of some and the removal of others of the master spirits who guided it from this part of the country, to the frequency of the meetings, and the high rate at which the yearly subscription was fixed, and deprived of the fostering care and immediate superintendence of Bishop Macdonell by his removal to Kingston, the Society, after some years of usefulness, struggled for some time under all these difficulties (added to which were those imposed upon by political excitement and the private dissensions of some of its members) and then sank into the sleep from which the exertions of Mr. Macdonald of Gart (and, I presume, those of the then Secretary as well, although be sure he did not mention it !) awakened it.

That its first act on its reorganization was one worthy of the Scotch gentlemen who regulated its affairs and worthy of the great Highlander then lately departed, we shall shortly see.

The Bishop's Last Visit to England.

At the dinner given to him on the eve of his departure for England there was a large attendance of the Bishop's friends of all religious denominations, including nearly all the prominent residents of the city and the officers of the garrison, with whom the Bishop always lived on terms of the most intimate and cordial friendship.

The chair was taken by the Sheriff of the district, supported on either side by the Bishop and his coadjutor. The toasts and speeches usual on such occasions were given and made, and the affair passed off to the satisfaction of all present. Some days afterwards the Bishop commenced his journey, and was accompanied to the Steamboat " Dolphin " by a large number of his personal friends, the old bell of St. Joseph's Church pealing forth a parting salute.

The Bishop and his party landed at Liverpool on the 1st of August, 1839. Soon after his arrival the Bishop went to London, where he communicated personally with the Colonial Office regarding his plan of emigration from the Highlands as a measure of relief to his suffering fellow-countrymen in Scotland, and as a security and benefit to his fellow-countrymen in Canada ; as well as with regard to the establishing of the College for the domestic education of the priesthood and other matters. He then visited the scenes of his nativity and childhood, and was present at the great northern meeting at Inverness in October. In the same month he passed over to Ireland, intending to be present at a great dinner given to the Catholic prelates in the City of Cork, but a dense fog in the Clyde and adverse winds prevented him from arriving in time for the festival. Nevertheless, he visited the Bishops, and being unable to obtain, in the West of Ireland, any other conveyance than a jaunting car, he was exposed during the entire day to one of the drizzling rains so common to that region. This exposure brought on inflammation of the lungs, accompanied by a severe cough ; and although he placed himself under the care of the President of Carlow College, and afterwards with the Jesuits of Clongowes Wood, and received much benefit and every attention, he still continued so indisposed on arriving in Dublin as to be obliged to keep to his bed for nearly a fortnight. From Dublin he went to Armagh, and remained a short time with the Catholic Primate. He then accepted the invitation of his friend the Earl of Gosford, to Gosford Castle, near Market Hill, Armagh, where, under the roof of that kind-hearted nobleman, who had been Governor-General of Canada from 1835 to 1838 (immediately preceding the Earl of Durham), he appeared to have completely recovered. He then returned to Scotland, a great meeting of noblemen and proprietors having in the meantime been held (on the 10th of January, 1840) at the Hopetown Room, Edinburgh, at which the Bishop's measure of emigration was discussed, the Bishop's travelling companion, Dr. Rolph, attending it as his representative.

ILLNESS AND DEATH OF BISHOP MACDONELL.

The following account is given by the Reverend Æneas Macdonell Dawson, of Ottawa, then an inmate of the Mission House at Dumfries, Scotland, of the Bishop's last illness and death :—

"According to my recollection, the Bishop came to Dumfries, convalescent, from Lord Gosford's, in Ireland, where he had been most kindly treated, I may say, nursed by the family of the good ex-Governor of Canada. What made the journey difficult and hurtful was the circumstance that he was obliged to come all the way from Port Patrick to Dumfries outside the stage, the inner places having been previously engaged. It was a Saturday afternoon when he reached Dumfries, a cold Scotch rain having fallen npon him all the time of his slow journey of from seventy to eighty miles. This did not improve his health. He complained of fatigue and would not leave the hotel where he was set down till next morning, when he came to the Mission House and was able to celebrate Mass, assisted by the Venerable Mr. Reid. Unwilling to leave him alone at the hotel, we, that is Mr. Reid and I, resolved ourselves into a committee of the whole and decided that I should go to spend the evening with him at the hotel. He was cheerful and conversed a great deal, not forgetting to hold out every inducement for me to go with him to Canada. I could not then consent, but if he had lived a few weeks longer, it is possible that my destinies might have been changed. Next day, Colonel Sir William Gordon, a devoted friend of the Bishop, invited me to walk with him. The conversation turned chiefly on Canada, and he urged on me the propriety of complying with the Bishop's request, that I should devote myself to that interesting country. It was not, however, till after long service in my native land that I decided on coming to this New World. The Bishop continued apparently well, although we knew that he was not, as he could not go out without using a respirator. On the Monday evening, Mr. Reid remained in his room, conversing with him until about eleven o'clock. About four o'clock next morning he called his man, but, he not hearing, the housekeeper approached his room, and dreading all was not right, entered. He asked for an additional blanket, and that the fire should be stirred up. The blanket was speedily supplied, and the housekeeper hastened to inform Mr. Reid of the state of matters. He lost no time in coming to the Bishop, and fortunately he was in time to administer the last Sacrament. I was next alarmed, and I found Mr. Reid sitting in his canonicals by the Bishop's bedside. The latter was passing away so quietly, in perfect peace, that we could not tell whether the vital spark had flown; nor was it known until Dr. Blacklock arrived, and after due examination, pronounced. I then hastened to the hotel where his friend, Sir William Gordon, was staying. The latter came promptly, and arriving in the Bishop's room, threw himself into a chair and wept. There was no funeral at Dumfries : the remains were conveyed at once to Edinburgh. Bishop Gillies, with the full consent of the Senior Bishop, had everything arranged in the grandest style. Since the days of Scotland's Royalty. so magnificent a funeral had not been seen in Edinburgh. All that was mortal of the renowned Bishop was deposited in the crypt of St. Margaret's Convent Chapel. I may mention that on the Tuesday forenoon, Captain Lyon, of Kirkmichael, the husband of Miss Dickson, who was a ward of the Bishop, called at the Mission House in order to see that all were ready to attend the dinner he was to give next day at his beautiful seat in honour of the Bishop. We were all to rejoice, along with the neighboring country gentlemen, on the occasion of Bishop Macdonell's return to Scotland, but he was bidden to another banquet."

On the arrival at Kingston of the melancholy intelligence of the Bishop's death, a Solemn Requiem Mass was sung by Bishop Gaulin, who took formal possession of the See on Passion Sunday, 1840. The funeral oration on the deceased Prelate was pronounced from the text, Beati Mortui, &c., by the Bishop's old friend and Vicar-General, Mr. W. P. Macdonald. The Requiem was attended by all the Clergy of the Diocese, which comprised the entire Province of Canada West. Several Priests from abroad also assisted. The successors of Bishop Macdonell in the See of Kingston always cherished the intention of bringing his remains to Canada for in-terment with suitable honour in the Cathedral Church of his Diocese, where, by right, the remains of a Bishop should always be deposited. It was not, however, until 1861, during the Episcopate of Bishop Horan, that the removal took place. Bishop Horan went to Edin-burgh and was cordially received by the Vicar-Apostolic of the Eastern District of Scotland, the Right Reverend James Gillies, who gave him every facility for the accomplishment of his Mission. Of Scottish extraction, Bishop Gillies was a native of Montreal, and was at one time spoken of as the coadjutor to Bishop Macdonell. The funeral cortege arrived in Kingston on the 25th September. On the following day a Solemn Requiem Mass having been celebrated by Bishop Horan, and a panegyric pronounced by the Reverend Mr. Bentley, of Montreal, the earthly remains of the much loved and venerated prelate were consigned to their last resting-place, in the land of his adoption, among the people whom he so loved and cared for, and amongst whom he had spent the greater part of his active, laborious and self-sacrificing life.

The Bishop's Memory Honoured at St. Raphael's.

The Highland Society of Canada having been resuscitated, the then secretary, in his narrative, states :—

"It now becomes my pleasing task to speak of an act of the Society, the first public act since its reorganization, which was hailed with the highest degree of satisfaction, not alone by the Highlanders of Glengarry, but by all true-hearted British subjects in the United Provinces—the erection of a monument by it to the memory of the author of its existence—the late Bishop Macdonell.

" Were the Society to have revived solely for that purpose, and were it never to do another act from which good of any kind could be derived, I will be supported in advancing that it has already done enough to entitle it to the gratitude and best wishes of all Canadians, for it has spared them the possibility of other people turning upon them with scorn, to say, ' You have allowed him who was your warmest and best friend, whose long and valuable life was uninterruptedly devoted to your service, without distinction of your race or creed, to lay dead for upwards of three years, without your having gratitude enough among you to pay any—the slightest mark—of respect to his memory. Yes ! you accepted all that he could do for you, received all that he could give you, and when he died, and could give no more, you neglected his memory.'

" The day on which this monument was erected must be looked upon in Canada as a day to which no ordinary interest is attached; and will be forever remembered by being associated with the undying remembrance of him who has very appropriately been called ' the father of his people.' On it the Highland Society must ever look with peculiar satisfaction, as upon a day conferring lasting honour upon them ; and when those who now compose it and who were engaged in that day's good work, are gone where their illustrious founder has proceeded them, may their successors, by a continuance of the generous and patriotic feelings which governed that day, bear out the Reverend Mr. Urquhart in saying ' that while this was an act worthy of the new-being of the Society, it was an act auspicuous of its future character.'

" At a meeting of the Society at Cornwall on the 9th of May, 1843, over which the President presided, the Reverend Mr. Urquhart, to whom an acquaintance with that inestimable man, had endeared the memory of the Bishop, after some eloquent and most feeling remarks, introduced the following resolution, which being seconded by the Reverend George Alexander Hay, was put and carried unanimously :—

" Resolved, that the Highland Society of Canada do erect on the 18th of June next, in the Parish Church of St. Raphael's, a tablet to the memory of the late Bishop Alexander Macdonell; that the said Society meet on that day, which is the day of the festival anniversary meeting, at eleven o'clock at Macdonell's in Williamstown, and proceed thence at twelve o'clock in procession to the Parish Church, where the Reverend John Macdonald be requested to read prayers, to erect the tablet; and that George S. Jarvis, Esquire, Guy C. Wood, Esquire, and Alexander MacMartin, Esquire, be a committee to procure such tablet."

" A tablet of very beautiful workmanship, bearing the following inscription :—

"On the 18th of June, 1843,

" THE HIGHLAND SOCIETY OF CANADA

" Erected this Tablet to the memory of

"THE HONOURABLE AND RIGHT REVEREND
"ALEXANDER MACDONELL,

" BISHOP OF KINGSTON.

" Born 1760.   Died 1840.

" Though dead, he still lives in the hearts of his countrymen."

having been procured by the committee appointed for that purpose, was, under the direction of Mr. Macdonell, the Secretary (the compiler of this account) placed in the Church on Saturday, the 17th of June, to be ready against the coming of the Society on the following Monday, to witness its consecration by the Church.

"The members of the Society began to arrive at Williamstown about eleven o'clock on Monday, shortly after which a guard of honour from the 2nd Regiment of Glengarry Militia, under the command of Captain J. A. Macdonell (a grand-nephew of the late Bishop), arrived. At twelve, the Society and the immense multitude of the country people, whose respect for the memory of the late Bishop brought them together to witness the first mark of respect paid to His Lordship's memory in a country which owed so much to his exertions, and to honour the Society while so engaged, formed into a procession and took their way to St. Raphael's. When about half a mile out of the village they were met by the Very Reverend John Macdonald and his worthy colleague in the cause of religion, the Reverend Mr. Macdonald, of Alexandria, at the head of about three hundred men on horseback, who formed in rear of the procession, which they followed to St. Raphael's. Arriving at 'the corners,' the whole road between there and the Church, upwards of a mile, was found to be lined with green bushes, and arches every now and then; and the moment the procession passed under the first arch, an artillery detachment from the 2nd Regiment Glengarry Militia commenced firing minute guns, which they continued until it had arrived at the Church, where it was received by an immense concourse of people, composed of persons of all ranks, politics and religion, and in which members of the fair sex were to be seen intermingled with stout and stalwart Highlanders.

"Nothing could be finer than the effect the tout ensemble had ; yet though the whole country turned out to pay one mark of respect to the memory of their friend, even this was a slight acknowledgment of all the Bishop had done for his countrymen.

"From the door of the Church the President addressed the assemblage as nearly as I can recollect in these words :—

" 'As President of the Highland Society of Canada, I feel myself called upon to make some observations with respect to the interesting occasion which has brought us this day together at this place, and I regret much my inability to do so, as I could wish. We must all feel an inward satisfaction that the first of the Society's acts since its reorganization has been the erection of this tablet to the memory of a man whose loss to the country we must all deplore.

" ' The late Bishop Macdonell was in all respects an uncommon man ; one of those whom we see rise up in an age to advance the good of mankind and elevate our conception of human nature ; he was, in a word, a great and good man. His private virtues endeared him to all who had the pleasure of his acquaintance, and his exalted patriotism and devoted loyalty to his Sovereign will long cause his name to be cherished at home and abroad. I may truly say that no one ever had the honour and prosperity of his country more truly at heart than his late Lordship ; and although this tribute to his memory is small and of little value, when compared with his great worth, it is to be hoped that generations to come will appreciate the motives from which it originated. This solemn ceremony—this first act of our revived Society—must, I am convinced, be highly approved of wherever this worthy man and true Christian was known.

" ' To Glengarry, in particular, where the prime of his valuable life was spent, and for the prosperity of which and to maintain the honour and elevate the character of whose people all the energies of his mind were ever directed, this day must indeed be gratifying ; and I trust that I shall live to see the day when a grateful people shall erect in this place a monument worthy of his memory, to which the passer-by may point, and pointing say, " HERE WERE SPENT THE BEST DAYS OF BISHOP MACDONELL, THE FATHER OF HIS PEOPLE."

" ' We all know his great anxiety to preserve in this country the language and genuine character of the Highlanders. He early con-ceived the idea of forming here a Highland Society, and with that object in view he procured from the Highland Society of London the Commission under which we now act; of the Society thus formed he continued to fill the presidential chair with much ease and dignity while it remained in active operation. All those associated with him in that Commission, with the exception of the humble individual who now addresses you, are now no more, but they all live in our memories—and one of them in particular, as the dear and sincere friend of the late Bishop—the Honourable William MacGillivray, whose cordial co-operation and generous liberality contributed so much to the formation of the Society—may, I trust, without any irreverence, have his name associated with this day's work.

" ' I will not detain you any longer by enlarging on the character of this inestimable Prelate ; it will remain for future historians to give it to posterity, with those of other eminent men of his day ; and I will conclude by hoping that we may all follow the example of our departed friend and lamented President in promoting the objects of our Society with zeal, harmony and cordiality, and, by so doing, confer a benefit on our country and reflect credit on ourselves.'

" The President having ceased speaking, the bell rang for church where the Vicar-General delivered a short but impressive discourse. The Honourable Mr. MacGillivray addressed the people in the Gaelic language on their coming out, but I regret being unable to give his speech (which, from the impression it seemed to make upon his hearers, must have been worthy of him) being, I am ashamed to say, unacquainted with the language in which it was delivered. Everything being over, the Society returned to Williamstown under a salute of ten guns, carrying with it the conviction that in Glengarry there was a field worthy of its best exertions."

Had the Bishop had a voice in the direction of the mark of respect thus shown to him, he could scarcely have wished or planned it otherwise than as it was performed. No man gloried more in his country than did he, there never was a truer Briton ; the ever memorable 18th of June was therefore a day ever dear to him : again, though a Catholic Priest and a Catholic Prelate, he always respected other men's convictions, and was in return respected by those who differed from him in religion ; witness the fact that it was Dr. Urquhart, for many years the leading Presbyterian Minister of this part of Upper Canada, who moved the resolution suggesting the erection of the tablet, and three gentlemen of the Protestant faith who were appointed to select it ; it emanated from the Highland Society of the

Province, which he had originated and for years presided over, and the tribute to his memory was placed in the Church of the Parish where the greater portion of his life was spent, and whose people, kinsmen, clansmen and fellow-countrymen he had served so faithfully, the two chief speakers on the occasion, Mr. Macdonald of Gart and Mr. MacGillivray, being both Presbyterians.

Obituary Notices.

I shall conclude this imperfect sketch of the Bishop's life by quoting from one of the secular papers of the time (the Kingston "British Whig"), and the conclusion of Mr. Morgan's reference to him in his "Biographies of Celebrated Canadians." The "Whig's" article was as follows :—

"Of the individuals who have passed away from us during the last twenty-five years, and who have taken an interest in the advancement and prosperity of Canada West, no one probably has won for himself in so great a degree the esteem of all classes of his fellow-citizens as has Bishop Macdonell.

"Arriving in Canada at an early period of the present century, at a time when toil, privations and difficulties inseparable from life in a new country, awaited the zealous Missionary as well as the hardy immigrant, he devoted himself in a noble spirit of self-sacrifice, and with untiring energy, to the duties of his sacred calling and the amelioration of the condition of those entrusted to his spiritual care. In him they found a friend and counsellor ; to them he endeared himself through his unbounded benevolence and greatness of soul. Moving among all classes and creeds, with a mind unbiassed by religious prejudices, taking an interest in all that tended to develope the resources, or aided the general prosperity of the country, he acquired a popularity still memorable, and obtained over the mind of his fellow-citizens an influence only equalled by their esteem and respect for him. The ripe scholar, the polished

gentleman, the learned divine, his many estimable qualities recommended him to the notice of the Court of Rome ; and he was
elevated to the dignity of a Bishop of the Catholic Church. The
position made no change in the man ; he remained still the zealous
Missionary, the indefatigable Pastor. His loyalty to the British
Crown was never surpassed ; when the interests of the Empire were
either assailed or jeopardized on this continent, he stood forth their
bold advocate ; by word and deed he proved how sincere was his
attachment to British Institutions ; and infused into the hearts of
his fellow-countrymen and others an equal enthusiasm for their preservation and maintenance. Indeed, his noble conduct on several
occasions tended so much to the preservation of loyalty that it drew
from the highest authority repeated expressions of thanks and
gratitude. As a member of the Legislative Council of Upper
Canada (to which he was called by Sir John Colborne on October
12th, 1831), his active mind, strengthened by experience acquired
by constant associations with all classes, enabled him to suggest
many things most beneficial to the best interests of the country, and
the peace and harmony of its inhabitants."

Mr. Morgan thus concludes his article —

" In every relation of life, as subject, Prelate, relative and
friend, he was a model of everything valuable. To his Sovereign
he brought the warm and hearty homage of a sincere, enthusiastic,
unconditional allegiance, and the most invincible, uncompromising
loyalty ; as Prelate, he was kind, attentive and devoted to the interests,
welfare and happiness of his Clergy ; as a relative, his attachment
was unbounded and his death created an aching void to hundreds of
sorrowing relatives whom he counselled by his advice, assisted with
his means and protected by his influence ; as a friend, he was
sincere, enthusiastic and unchangeable in his attachments. Such,
indeed, was the liberality of his views and the inexpressible benignity
of his disposition, that all creeds and classes united in admiration of
his character, respect for him, and congregated together to bid him
farewell as he left the shores of the St. Lawrence on that voyage,
which proved but the prelude to that long and last one, from which
there is no return."

The following beautiful verses, composed by Robert Gilfillan, a Scottish poet of some celebrity, appeared in the Edinburgh Weekly Chronicle at the time of the Bishop's funeral services there :—

DIRGE OF THE LATE BISHOP MACDONELL.

BY ROBERT GILFILLAN.

The temple was wrapt in deepest gloom,
As they laid out the dead for the silent tomb,
 And the tapers were lighted dim—
A soft and solemn shadowy light—
And the Book was opened for Holy Rite,
 When they woke this funeral hymn :
" He's gone ! he's gone ! the spirit is fled,
And now we mourn the honoured dead ! "

The coffin before the Altar stood,
With purple pall and silken shroud,
 And tassels sable hung,
And as they bore it slow along,
They chanted forth the burial song,
 By hundred voices sung—
" He's gone ! he's gone ! the spirit is fled,
And now we mourn the honoured dead ! "

And many a Priest with mitred brow,
Before the Holy Cross did bow,
 And joined the mournful strain.
" The living once !—the lifeless now !
All, all, to Death's fell grasp must bow,
 Nor come they back again ! "
The tide gives back its ebbing wave,
But there's no return from the darksome grave !

Frail mortals of a passing day,
Is this your home?   Is this your stay?
   Attend the lesson given;
'Tis dust to dust and clay to clay,
The friends we mourn from earth away,
   They welcome now in Heaven!"
'Twas thus they bore him slow along,
With Holy chant and mournful song.

They spoke of his deeds well done on earth,
His Holy life, and active worth,
   Relieving others' woe ;
The poor in him they found a friend,
Whose like again they will not find,
   In this cold world below !
Did good where good was to be done,
But his race is o'er, and the prize is won !

They chanted the Requiem in cadence deep—
The good may grieve, but the dead shall sleep,
   When life's dull round is o'er—
Rest, Pilgrim, from a distant land,
A peaceful home is now at hand,
   Where troubles come no more !
Like a shock of corn he ripely fell,
His days were long, but he used them well !

CHORUS.

Raise the crosier o'er the dead,
Chants are sung, and Mass is said ;
Bear him to the dwelling low
Where all sons of Adam go.
Sisters, brothers, onward come,
Earth is but a living tomb,
Full of sorrow, full of sadness,
Little joy, and little gladness ;
Listen what the Scripture saith,
" In midst of life we walk in death ! "

APPENDIX A.

The venerable and distinguished Institution mentioned in the text, the Highland Society of London, of which Bishop Macdonell was instrumental in establishing a branch in Canada, was founded in 1778, and·has always received the encouragement and approbation of the Sovereign and Princes of the Blood Royal.'

The interest which Her present Majesty takes and has ever taken in all that concerns Scotland is proverbial. But her predecessors of her line and other members of their Royal Family have been equally pronounced in their solicitude and respect for all that appertained to that portion of their Kingdom, the earlier of them indeed when men, reverenced by them and properly counted amongst the most devoted and loyal of their subjects still lived who had not hesitated to risk their lives and sacrifice their fortunes in another and an adverse though unfortunate Cause. How nobly they have been repaid, the history of Great Britain records.

In 1776, Mr. Pitt, afterwards the first and the great Earl of Chatham, in his celebrated speech on the commencement of the differences with America, was able to pronounce from his place in Parliament the following eulogy on the Jacobite clans :—

"I sought for merit wherever it could be found. It is my boast that I was the first Minister who looked for it, and found it in the Mountains of the North. I called it forth, and drew into your service a hardy and intrepid race of men ; men who left by your jealousy became a prey to the artifices of your enemies, and had gone nigh to have overturned the State in the war before last. These men in the last war were brought to combat on your side ; they served with fidelity as they fought with valor, and conquered for you in every quarter of the world."

Let me give the record of the Highlanders of the next generation. It shows that they had not degenerated.

From 1806 to 1814, gold medals were granted to officers who rendered conspicuous service in battles fought between those years. I take the official list and find that in the twenty-six battles for which they were granted those names occurring more than four times were all Scottish, with the exception of three.

The Battles and Actions for which gold medals were granted were as follows :—

1   Maida, 4 July, 1806.
2   Roleia, 17 August, 1808.
3   Vimiera, 21 August, 1808.
4   Sahagun, Benevente, &c. (Actions of Cavalry), December, 1808, and January, 1809.
5   Corunna, 16 January, 1809.
6   Martinique, Attack and Capture, February, 1809.
7   Talavera de la Reyna, 27 and 28 July, 1809.
8   Guadaloupe, Attack and Capture, January and Feb., 1810.
9   Busaco, 27 September, 1810.
10   Barrosa, March 5, 1811.
11   Fuentes D'Onor, 5 May, 1811.
12   Albuhera, 16 May, 1811.
13   Java, Attack and Capture, August and September, 1811.
14   Ciudad Rodrigo, Assault and Capture, January and February, 1812.
15   Badajoz, Assault and Capture, 11 March and 6 April, 1812.
16   Salamanca, 22 July, 1812.
17   Fort Detroit, Capture of, America, August, 1812.
18   Vittoria, 21 June, 1813.
19   Pyrenees, 28 July to 2 August, 1813.
20   St. Sebastian, Assault and Capture, August and September, 1813.
21   Chateauguay, America, 26 October, 1813.
22   Nivelle, 10 November, 1813.
23   Chrystler's Farm, America, 11 November, 1813.
24   Nive, 9 to 13 December, 1813.
25   Orthes, 27 February, 1814.
26   Toulouse, 10 April, 1814.

The following are the names occurring more than three times in the list, with the rank of the officers subsequently attained or held at time of death, when killed, and battles or actions for which the medals were granted :— §

Cameron, Lt.-Gen. Sir Alan, K.C.B., 79 F., died in 1828 (7).

†Cameron, Maj.-Gen. Sir Alex., K.C.B., 74 F., died in 1850 (14, 15, 16).

Cameron, Lt.-Col. Charles, 3 F., died in 1827 (22, 24).

Cameron, Lt.-Gen. Sir John, K.C.B., 9 F., died in 1844 (3, 5, 9, 16, 18, 20, 24).

Cameron, Col. John, 92 F., killed 18 June, 1815 (18, 24, 25).

Cameron, Lt.-Col. Phillip, 79 F., died in 1811 (5).

Campbell, Lt.-Gen. Sir Alex., Bart, K.C.B., 80 F., died in 1825 (7).

Campbell, Lt.-Col. Alex. Wm., Port. Serv., died in 1813 (12, 18).

Campbell, Maj.-Gen. Archibald, C.B., died in 1838 (6, 18).

Campbell, Col. Archibald, 46 F., died in 1840 (24).

Campbell, Lt.-Gen. Sir Archibald, G.C.B., 62 F., died in 1843 (12, 18, 19, 22, 24).

*Campbell, Lt.-Col. Charles Stuart, C.B., h.p., 1 F. (18, 20).

†Campbell, Lt.-Gen. Sir Colin, K.C.B., 72 F., died in 1847 (7, 9, 11, 15, 16, 18, 19, 22, 24, 26).

†Campbell, Lt.-Col. Colin, C.B., 34 F., died in 1833 (16, 18).

Campbell, Major Duncan, 39 F., died in 1823 (19).

Campbell, Lt.-Col., F.B., h. p. unatt., died in 1827 (25).

†*Campbell, Major-Gen. Sir Guy, Bart., C.B., died in 1848 (19).

Campbell, Gen. Sir Henry Fred, K.C.B., G.C.H., 25 F (7, 16).

Campbell, Major-Gen. Sir James, K.C.B., K.C.H., 74 Foot, died in 1835 (11, 14, 15, 16, 18).

§The figures annexed to the name show the actions at which the officer was present. One gold medal only was granted for Roleia and Vimiera (2 and 3).

Those officers who had received honorary distinctions for four actions had a cross, and a clasp was added for each subsequent action.

The officers marked * have received silver medals for other actions, while † indicated that the officer had also received the Waterloo medal.

†Campbell, Col. John, C.B., 42 F., died in 1841 (25, 26).

†Campbell, Major-Gen. Sir Neil, Royal Af. Corps, died in 1827 (6, 8, 14, 16).

†Campbell, Brev. Lieut.-Col. Patrick, C.B., h.p. unatt., died in 1850 (22, 24).

Campbell, Lt.-Col. Robert, h.p., 28 F. (20).

Campbell, Lt.-Col. Wm., 78 F., died of wounds in 1811 (13).

Campbell, Major Wm., h.p. unatt., died in 1840 (19, 22).

Douglas, Lt.-Gen. Sir James, K.C.B., 42 F. (9, 16, 19, 22, 24, 25, 26).

†*Douglas, Lt.-Gen. Sir Neil, K.C.B., K.C.H., 72 F. (19, 22, 24, 26).

Douglas, Col. Robert, C.B., R. Art. (16, 18, 19, 22).

Douglas, Col. Sir William, K.C.B., 91 F., died in 1818 (5, 19, 22, 24, 25, 26).

Fraser, Maj. James, 78 F., died in 1813 (13).

Fraser, Lt.-Gen. Mackenzie, died in 1809 (5).

Fraser, Maj. Peter, 1 F., killed in 1813 (18).

†Fraser, Col. Sir Augustus, K.C.B., R. Art., died in 1835 (18, 20, 22, 24, 26).

Gordon, Lt.-Col. Hon. A., aide-de-camp, killed in action (16, 18, 19, 22, 24, 25, 26).

Gordon, Lt.-Col. Alex., 83 F., killed in 1809 (7).

Gordon, Gen. Gabriel, 91 F. (6, 8).

Gordon, Major-Gen. Sir Leger, 8 W. I. Reg., died in 1810 (5).

Gordon, Lt.-Col. John, 1 F., died in 1814 (9).

*Gordon, Major-Gen. Wm. A., C.B., 54 F. (24).

Gordon, Capt. W., h.p. Port. Service, died in 1834 (20).

Gordon, Capt. Wm., h.p. 6 W. I. Regt., died in 1821 (20).

†Grant, Lt.-Gen. Sir Colquhoun, K.C.B., G.C.H., 15 Dr., died in 1836 (4, 18).

Grant, Lt.-Col. Sir Maxwell, K.C.B., h.p. Port. Serv., died in 1823 (18, 19, 22, 24, 25).

Grant, Lt.-Col. Peter, C.B., E. I. Co. Serv., died in 1816 (13).

Grant, Major-Gen. Wm., died in 1826 (18, 19).

Hill, Col. Chas., C.B., 50 F., died in 1819 (18).

Hill, Major-Gen. Sir Dudley St. Ledger, K.C.B. (11, 15, 16, 18, 20).

†Hill, Lt.-Col. J. H. E., C.B., 49 F., died in 1838 (16, 20, 22, 24).

†*Hill, Col. Sir Robert C., C.B., Royal Horse Guards (18).

†Hill, Gen. Rowland Viscount, G.C.B., K.C.H., K.C., died in 1842 (2, 3, 5, 7, 18, 19, 22, 24, 25).

†Hill, Col. Sir Thomas Noel, K.C.B., 13 Dr., died in 1832 (9, 14, 16, 18, 20).

King, Major George, 7 F., killed in 1815 (15).

King, Lt.-Gen. Sir Henry, C.B., K.C.H., 3 F. (18).

King, Lt.-Gen. Hon. Sir Henry, K.C.B., 1 W. I. Regt., died in 1839 (9, 16).

King, Lt. J. G. Maj., Port. Serv., died in 1816 (25).

Macdonald, Col. Duncan, 57 F. (18, 19, 22).

*Macdonald, Major-Gen. John, C.B., (18, 19).

Macdonald, Lt.-Gen. Sir John, G.C.B., 42 F. (10, 24).

Macdonald, Lt.-Col. Robert, C.B., R. Art. (16).

Macdonell, Major Arch., 92 F., killed in 1813 (11).

Macdonell, Lt.-Col. Donald, Port. Serv., killed in 1812 (12, 15).

Macdonell, Lt.-Col. John, Canadian Militia, killed in 1812 (17).

†*Macdonell, Lt.-Gen. Sir James, K.C.B., K.C.H., 79 F. (1).

Macdonell, Lt.-Col. George, C.B., 79 F., (21).

Macdonell, Lt.-Col. Chichester, 82 F., died in 1811 (5).

Mackenzie, Col. Colin, Madras Eng., died in 1821 (13).

Mackenzie, Major-Gen. J. R., killed in 1809 (7).

Mackenzie, Lt-Col. J. W., 5 F., killed in 1809 (2, 3).

Mackenzie, Major Maxwell, 71 F., killed in 1813 (18).

Macleod, Lt.-Col. Thomas, 78 F., killed in 1807 (1).

Macleod, Col. Alex, C.B., 59 F., died in 1821 (13).

Macleod, Lt.-Col. Chas., 43 F., killed in 1812 (9, 14, 15).

Macleod, Lt.-Col. Wm., 69 F., killed in 1811 (13).

Napier, Lt.-Col. Alex., 92 F., killed in 1809 (5).

*Napier, Lt.-Gen. Sir Charles James, G.C.B., 22 F. (5).

*Napier, Lt.-Gen. Sir George Thomas, K.C.B., 1 W. I. R. (6, 14).

*Napier, Major-Gen. Sir William F. P., K.C.B., 27 F. (16, 22, 24).

Napier, Lt.-Gen. Mark, died in 1843 (8).

Ross, Lt.-Col. Arch., h.p. Port. serv., died in 1826 (18).
†*Ross, Major-Gen. Sir Hew Dalrymple, K.C.B., R. Art (9, 15, 16, 18, 22, 24).
Ross, Lt.-Gen. John, C.B., died in 1843 (3).
Ross, Lt.-Col. John, 28 F (24, 25).
†Ross, Major-Gen. Sir John, K.C.B., died in 1835 (10, 18, 25, 26).
Ross, Major-General Robert, 20 F., killed in 1814 (1, 5, 18, 19, 25.)

*Smith, Major-Gen. Sir Charles Felix, K.C.B., R. Eng. (18, 20).
Smith, Major-Gen. Haviland, died in 1817 (1).
†*Smith, Major-Gen. James Webber, C.B., R. Art. (18, 20).
Smith, Col. Wm., 50 F., died in 1833 (9).

Stewart, Major-Gen. David, C.B., died in 1830 (1, 8).
Stewart, Capt. G., 42 F., killed in 1814 (24).
Stewart, Lt.-Col. Hon. James, C.B., Scotch Fus. Gds., died in 1836 (16, 18).
Stewart, Lt.-Col. John, 9 F., killed in 1813 (2).
Stewart, Lieut.-Col. John, 25 F., died in 1810 (8).
Stewart, Major John, 95 F., died of wounds 1811 (9).
Stewart, Brig.-Gen. Richard, died in 1810 (7).
Stewart, Lt.-Gen. Hon. Sir W., G.C.B., Rifle Brigade, died in 1826 (12, 18, 19, 22, 24, 25).
Stewart, Major-Gen. Wm., C.B., 40 F., died in 1836 (8).
Stewart, Major-Cen. Wm., 3 F. (12).

The other distinctively Highland names appearing in that Roll of Honour are: Bruce (1), Carmichael (1), Carr (1), Crauford (2), Crawford (1), Cumming (1), Drummond (2), Duncan (1), Forbes (2), Hay (2), Lindsay (1), MacComb (1), MacCreagh (1), MacIntosh (1), McNair (1), Macpherson (2), Macara (1), Macbean (1), Mackie (1), Maclean (3), Macneil (1), Mitchell (2), Morrison (2), Murray (3), Ramsay (3), Ray (1), Robertson (1), Scott (2), Shaw (1), Stuart (2), Wallace (1).

The "Ettrick Shepherd's" Dedication of His "Relics."

When His Royal Highness the Duke of York was President of the Highland Society in 1819, and in the chair, another Royal Duke being also present, it was determined that an effort should be made to rescue from oblivion the Jacobite songs.

The task was assigned to James Hogg, "the Ettrick Shepherd," whose labours culminated in the publication of "The Jacobite Relics" in the same year.

The dedication of his work was as follows :—

TO THE

MOST NOBLE AND HONOURABLE PRESIDENT AND MEMBERS

OF THE

HIGHLAND SOCIETY OF LONDON.

To the sons of the men who ne'er flinched from their faith,
But stood for their Sovereign to ruin and death,
These Songs I consign, as memorials that tell
Of the poets that sung, and the heroes that fell,
Whom interest ne'er moved their true King to betray,
Whom threat'ning ne'er daunted, nor power could dismay :
They stood to the last, and, when standing was o'er,
All sullen and silent they dropped the claymore,
And yielded indignant their necks to the blow,
Their homes to the flame, and their lands to the foe.
  Then flowed the wild strains to the rock and the wood,
Of the fall of the mighty, the Royal, and good ;
So plaintive and sweet, all were moved by the tone,
From the child of the cot to the Prince on the Throne :

The fates of the heroes they learned to deplore,
For our rocks never echoed such wailings before.
These strains, which a Shepherd has travailled to save,
With joy he consigns to the sons of the brave :
He lov'd them when fancy was ardent and young,
Even then of the Clans of the Highlands he sung ;
And oft has he journeyed the dwellings to view,
And the graves of the heroes so gallant and true :
Yes, oft o'er their mountains, unnoted, unknown
All weary and barefoot he wandered alone ;
For his Whiggish heart, with its Covenant tie,
Was knit to the Highlands, he could not tell why—
Was knit to the cause they espoused to their cost,
And grieved that the name of the STUART was lost !
    Then blest be the hands that have pointed the way
To rescue these relics from utter decay !
On the brink of oblivion all trembling they hung,
To die with the names of the loyal that sung ;
And wild though they be to the ear and the eye,
They still are the carols of ages gone by,
The strains of our country, unshackled and strong,
The lays of the land of proud honour and song.
    When Kings were degraded, to ruffians a prey,
Or driven from the Thrones of their fathers away,
Who then could sit silent ?   Alas for the while,
That now there are myriads, the worst of the vile,
Whose highest ambition is bent to defame
All greatness and Sovereignty, order and name !
But whether in high or in humble degree,
My country, such spirit dishonours not thee !
    Ah woe to the Nation, its honour falls low,
When mendicant meddlers dare Majesty brow,
And turn up the snout of derision and scorn
At those who to honour or titles are born !
All beggarly power is the bane of mankind :
" It leads to bewilder, and dazzles to blind."

And now, Noble Highlanders, sons of the North,
That land of blue mountains, and birth-place of worth,
These strains that were chanted o'er many a wild heath,
These strains of your fathers, to you I bequeath ;
And with them this blessing, the best that I may :
OH, LONG BE YOU LOYAL AND GALLANT AS THEY !

The Ettrick Shepherd, in his introductory chapter, gives some incidents which may perhaps astonish some of the present generation who know little and perhaps would care less to know of the views entertained by Her Majesty's predecessors with regard to these matters. For instance, writing, as I have mentioned, in the year 1819, he states :—

" When the Princess of Wales, mother of His present Majesty, mentioned, with some appearance of censure, the conduct of Lady Margaret Macdonald, who harboured and concealed Prince Charles, when, in the extremity of peril, he threw himself on her protection ; 'and would not you, madam,' answered Prince Frederick, 'have done the same in the same circumstances ? I am sure—I hope in God you would.' Besides the great measure of restoring the forfeited estates to the Chiefs, our venerable Sovereign showed on every occasion, how little his heart was capable of nourishing any dislike against those who had acted against the authority of his house. The support which he afforded to the exiled branch of the Stuarts will form a bright trait in his history. * * * His Majesty having been told of a gentleman of family and fortune in Perthshire who had not only refused to take the oath of allegiance to him, but had never permitted him to be named as King in his presence. 'Carry my compliments to him,' said the King, 'but—what—stop—no— ; he may perhaps not receive my compliments as King of England. Give him the Elector of Hanover's compliments, and tell him that he respects the steadiness of his principles.' The same kindness to the memory of those who hazarded themselves in the cause of the Stuarts has been inherited by the present administrator of Royal authority; and to him, as to his father, their descendants have ever been prompt to repay it. He was heard to express himself one day before a dozen of gentlemen of both nations, with the greatest warmth, as follows :

' I have always regarded the attachment of the Scots to the Pretender —I beg your pardon, gentlemen—to Prince Charles Stuart, I mean —AS A LESSON TO ME WHOM TO TRUST IN THE HOUR OF NEED.' "

Mr. Hogg then mentions that the first proposal for rescuing the Jacobite relics from oblivion emanated from the Royal Family, and adds that the singular remark of Captain Stuart of Invernahoyle was not, it would seem, quite without foundation. A gentleman, in a large company, gibed him for holding the King's Commission, while at the same time he was a professed Jacobite. " So I may well be," answered Invernahoyle, " in imitation of my master. The King himself is a Jacobite." The gentleman shook his head, and remarked that the thing was impossible. " By God," said Stuart, " but I tell you he is, and every son he has. There is not one of them who if he had lived in my brave father's days would not to a certainty have been hanged."

The monument erected to Prince Charles Edward Stuart, his Royal Father and brother by King George IV., sculptured by Canova and placed in St. Peter's Church in Rome, is, as stated by Mr. Aytoun, the most graceful tribute ever paid by Royalty to misfortune : REGIO CINERI PIETAS REGIA.

It was the justification of the Jacobites when the Cause was ended forever.

It was surmounted by the Royal Arms of Great Britain, and the inscription was as follows :—

JACOBO III.

JACOBI II MAGNÆ BRIT. REGIS FILIO

KAROLO EDVARDO

ET

HENRICO

DECANO PATRUM CARDINALUM

JACOBI III FILIIS

REGIÆ STIRPIS STUARDIÆ POSTREMIS

ANNO MDCCCXIX.

———

BEATI MORTUI

QUI IN DOMINO MORIUNTUR.

APPENDIX B.

Bishop Macdonell used constantly to declare that every gentleman of his name should be either a priest or a soldier.

I have compiled a list of the officers of the name who have served in Canada in the regular service and militia during critical periods, from official sources and family records. It shows that the men of Glengarry's clan, perhaps the most pronounced of all the Jacobites, have done their share to implant and to uphold British Institutions in this part of the British Dominions, and that—to use the expression of the Prince Regent—they were to be trusted in the hour of need !

TAKING OF LOUISBURG, 1758.

TAKING OF QUEBEC.

BATTLE OF THE HEIGHTS OF ABRAHAM, 1759.

1. John Macdonell (Lochgarry)—Captain 78th Regiment (Fraser's Highlanders) ; afterwards Colonel 76th Regiment (Macdonald Highlanders) ; wounded at the taking of Quebec. (Had previously served in the Garde Ecossaise, Ogilvie's Corps, after Culloden. The attainder was levied in his favour).

2. Charles Macdonell, son of Glengarry—Captain 78th Regiment (Fraser's Highlanders) ; wounded at the Battle of the Heights of Abraham ; killed at the capture of St. John's, Newfoundland.

3. Ranald Macdonell, son of Keppoch—Lieutenant 78th Regiment (Fraser's Highlanders) ; wounded at the taking of Quebec.

4. William Macdonell—Lieutenant 78th Regiment (Fraser's Highlanders).

5. John Macdonell (Leek)—Lieutenant 78th Regiment (Fraser's Highlanders) ; wounded at the taking of Louisburg ; served through the Revolutionary War ; died a Colonel in the

service. (He had been on the staff of Prince Charles Stuart in 1745, and was twice wounded at Culloden).

6. Alexander Macdonell (son of Barrisdale)—Lieutenant 78th Regiment (Fraser's Highlanders) ; killed at the taking of Quebec.

REVOLUTIONARY WAR 1776-83.

7. Alexander Macdonell (Aberchalder)—Captain 1st Battalion King's Royal Regiment of New York—8 years. (Had been an Aide-de-Camp to Prince Charles Stuart in 1745).

8. Angus Macdonell—Captain 1st Battalion King's Royal Regiment of New York (Ensign in 60th Regiment 8th July, 1760; Lieutenant in same 27th December, 1770—25 years.

9. John Macdonell (Younger of Aberchalder), Vide 22—Captain Butler's Rangers—5 years and 10 months. (Entered the service at the commencement of the War as Ensign and was subsequently Lieutenant in 84th Royal Highland Emigrant Regiment—3 years and 2 months ; afterwards Lieutenant-Colonel 2nd Battalion R.C.V. Regiment of Foot).

10. John Macdonell (of the family of Scothouse)—Captain 1st Battalion King's Royal Regiment of New York—8 years. (Had previously been in the Spanish army and was "out" in 1745).

11. Archibald Macdonell (of the family of Leek)—Captain 1st Battalion King's Royal Regiment of New York—8 years (afterwards Lieutenant of the County of Stormont and Colonel Stormont Militia).

12. James Macdonell—Captain 2nd Battalion King's Royal Regiment of New York—8 years.

13. Allan Macdonell (of the family of Leek)—Captain-Lieutenant 1st Battalion Royal Regiment of New York—8 years.

14. Alexander Macdonell (Younger of Collachie, whose father and mother were prisoners of War to the Americans)—First-Lieutenant Butler's Rangers. (Entered the service as a Cadet in the King's Royal Regiment of New York. Served

also as Ensign in 84th Royal Highland Emigrants)—7 years.

15. Hugh Macdonell, son of Aberchalder, Vide 23—Lieutenant 1st Battalion King's Royal Regiment of New York—7 years. Under date Chelsea College, 23rd June, 1804, Colonel Mathews, for many years Military Secretary to Sir Frederick Haldimand and Sir Guy Cartier (Lord Dorchester) wrote as follows to the Under Secretary of State for War concerning this officer and his relatives mentioned in this list :—

" * * * His father and uncle left Scotland with their families and considerable property a few years before the rebellion in America, with a view to establish themselves in that country, having for that purpose carried out a number of their dependants. They obtained a valuable grant of land from Sir John Johnson on the Mohawk River, in the settlement of which they had made considerable progress.

" When the rebellion broke out, they were the first to fly to arms on the part of the Government, in which they and their adherents—not less than 200 men—took a most active and decided lead, leaving their families and property at the mercy of the rebels.

" I was at that time quartered at Niagara, and an eye witness of the gallant and successful exertions of the Macdonells and their dependants, by which, in a great measure, the Upper Country of Canada was preserved, for on this little body a very fine battalion was soon formed and afterwards a second." [R. R. N. Y., 1st and 2nd Batt.]

" Captain Macdonell's father and uncle, at that time advanced in years, had companies in that corps, and in which his elder brother " (No. 9) " afterwards an active and distinguished partizan, carried arms. The sons of both families, five or six in number, the moment they could bear arms, followed the bright example of their fathers, and soon became active and useful officers in that and another corps of Rangers" (Butler's) "whose strength and services greatly contributed to unite the Indians of the Five Nations in the interest of Government, and thereby decidedly to save the Upper Country of Canada and our Indian trade."

16. Ranald Macdonell—Lieutenant 84th Regiment (Royal Highland Emigrants)—8 years and 4 months (formerly in 17th Regiment).

17. Archibald Macdonell—Lieutenant 84th Regiment (Royal Highland Emigrants).

18. Angus Macdonell—Lieutenant 74th Regiment.

19. Chichester Macdonell (son of Aberchalder) — 2nd Lieutenant Butler's Rangers—6 years. (Afterwards commanded 82nd Regiment of Foot). Gold medal for Corunna. Died on service in India.

20. Miles Macdonell (of the family of Scothouse)—Lieutenant 1st Battalion King's Royal Regiment of New York—2 years. (Afterwards Captain 2nd Battalion R.C.V. Regiment of Foot)

21. Ranald Macdonell (of the family of Leek)—Lieutenant 2nd Battalion King's Royal Regiment of New York—3 years.

2ND BATTALION ROYAL CANADIAN VOLUNTEER REGIMENT OF FOOT.

The first Regiment raised in Upper Canada (1796). Head-quarters, Fort George. Detachments at Fort Chippewa, Fort Erie, Amherstburg, Kingston and St. Joseph's Island, on service continually until disbanded with all other Fencible Regiments during the Peace of Amiens, 1802.

22. John Macdonell (Aberchalder) (No. 9)—Lieutenant-Colonel ; Colonel commanding Glengarry Militia Regiment 1803, and Lieutenant of the County of Glengarry. One of the two first members for Glengarry 1792, and Speaker of the first House of Assembly of Upper Canada.

23. Hugh Macdonell (No. 15)—Captain ; subsequently Senior Captain 1st Battalion R.C.V.; Lieutenant-Colonel Glengarry Militia 1803 ; first Adjutant-General of Militia Upper Canada ;

Assistant Commissary-General at Gibraltar 1805 ; His Majesty's Consul-General at Algiers 1811-20. (One of the first two members for Glengarry 1792). " His Royal Highness " (the Duke of Kent) "has always understood from those who have had occasion to be acquainted with his proceedings at Algiers, that his conduct has invariably met with the highest appreciation of Government for the judgment and firmness he has evinced in the most trying moments, a circumstance particularly gratifying to the Duke, who reflects with pleasure upon his being the first who brought him forward." Extract from a letter written by Lieutenant-Colonel Harvey, by command of H.R.H. the Duke of Kent at the time of Mr. Macdonell's death.

24. Miles Macdonell (No. 20)—Captain (afterwards Governor of Assiniboia in Lord Selkirk's Company).

25. Ranald Macdonell (No. 16)—Lieutenant.

26. Angus Macdonell—Lieutenant.

WAR OF 1812-14.

27. John Macdonell (son of Greenfield)—Lieutenant-Colonel Militia ; Aide-de-Camp and Military Secretary to Major General Sir Isaac Brock, K.B. Negotiated on behalf of His Majesty's Force, the terms of the Capitulation of Fort Detroit by the Americans August 16, 1812 ; gold medal for Taking of Detroit; killed at Queenston Heights October 13, 1812, æt. 27 ; member for Glengarry, and Attorney-General of Upper Canada at the time of his death.

" His Royal Highness has been pleased also to express his regret at the loss which the Province must experience in the death of the Attorney General, Mr. Macdonell, whose zealous co-operation with Sir Isaac Brock will reflect lasting honour on his memory." Extract of a despatch from the Right Honourable Earl Bathurst, one of His Majesty's principal Secretaries of State, to His Excellency Lieutenant-General Sir George Prevost, Bart., dated Downing Street, 8th December, 1812.

In communicating the above to Alexander Macdonell

of Greenfield, the father of the Attorney-General, Lieutenant-Colonel Coffin, Provincial A.D.C., under date York, March 20th, 1813, stated by command of His Honour the President that "it would doubtless afford some satisfaction to all the members of the family of which the late Attorney-General was so great an ornament to learn that his merit has been recognized even by the Royal personage, who wields the sceptre of the British Empire : on which His Honour commands me to declare his personal gratification."

28. George Macdonell (of the family of Leek)—Captain 8th (King's) Regiment ; Major Glengarry Light Infantry Regiment, which Regiment was raised by him and the Reverend Alexander Macdonell ; commanded at the Capture of Ogdensburg February 23, 1813 ; second in command at Battle of Chateauguay ; gold medal for Chateauguay ; C.B., 3rd February, 1817 ; Lieutenant-Colonel 79th Regiment.

29. The Reverend Alexander Macdonell—Chaplain Glengarry Light Infantry Regiment, formerly Chaplain Glengarry Fencible (British Highland) Regiment. (The first Catholic Chaplain in the British Army, and first Catholic Bishop of Upper Canada ; was largely instrumental in raising both the above Regiments.)

30. Angus Macdonell—Ensign Glengarry Light Infantry Regiment.

31. Alexander Macdonell—Ensign Glengarry Light Infantry Regiment.

32. Alexander Macdonell (Collachie) (No. 14)—Lieutenant-Colonel Militia, and Deputy Paymaster-General Militia ; made Prisoner of War at Capture of Niagara 26th May, 1813. (Member for Glengarry and Speaker House of Assembly 1804, afterwards member Legislative Council of Upper Canada).

33. Forbes Macdonell—Captain 10th Royal Veteran Battalion.

34. A. C. Macdonell—Ensign 104th (New Brunswick) Regiment.

35. Ranald Macdonell—Lieutenant Canadian Fencible Regiment.

36. Alexander Macdonell (Greenfield)—Lieutenant-Colonel 2nd Regiment Glengarry Militia.
37. Duncan Macdonell (Younger of Greenfield)—Captain 1st Regiment Glengarry Militia.
38. James Macdonell (of the family of Leek)—Ensign 1st Regiment Glengarry Militia.
39. Donald Macdonell (son of Greenfield)—Captain 2nd Regiment Glengarry Militia ; Assistant Quartermaster-General Midland District.
40. Alexander Macdonell—Ensign 2nd Regiment Glengarry Militia.
41. John Macdonell (of the family of Leek)—Lieutenant Incorporated Militia ; wounded at Lundy's Lane ; died of wounds at York.
42. John Macdonell (of the family of Leek)—Captain Incorporated Militia.
43. James Macdonell—Ensign Nova Scotia Fencible Regiment.

SUPPRESSION OF REBELLION IN UPPER AND LOWER CANADA, 1837-8.

44. Sir James Macdonell (Brother of Glengarry) — Lieutenant-General, K.C.B., K.C.H. ; commanding Brigade of Guards, and second in command of Her Majesty's Forces during the Rebellion ; appointed a Member of Lord Durham's Special Council 28th June, 1838. Lieutenant-Colonel Coldstream Guards at Waterloo, where he defended Hougomont. Colonel 79th Highlanders 14th July, 1842. Gold medal for Maida ; Waterloo medal ; medal and clasps for Salamanca, Vittoria, Nivelle and the Nive ; Order of Maria Theresa and a Knight (4th class) of St. Vladimir ; Principal Equerry to the Queen Dowager.
45. Donald Macdonell (of the family of Greenfield) (No. 39)—Colonel commanding 2nd Regiment Glengarry Militia. (Commission dated January 1st, 1822) ; raised by instructions of Lieutenant-General Sir John Colborne, K.C.B., commanding in Canada (dated 15th January, 1838), and commanded the Lancaster (2nd) Regiment of Glengarry Highlanders, which served in Lower Canada (at Napierville

and Beauharnois), and subsequently in Upper Canada. Deputy Adjutant-General of Militia Upper Canada 1846-61. Nominated by the Administrator of the Government to lay the Corner-stone of Brock's Monument on Queenston Heights, His Excellency expressing in General Order of 1st October, 1853, "his pleasure in nominating for this duty the brother of the gallant officer who fell nobly by the side of the Major-General in the performance of his duty as Provincial Aide-de-Camp." For many years Member for Glengarry.

46. Duncan Macdonell (Greenfield) (No. 36)—Lieutenant-Colonel 2nd Regiment Glengarry Militia. (Commission dated 1st January, 1822). Retired retaining rank 3rd September, 1857, the Commander-in-Chief declaring in General Orders of that date "his unwillingness to permit this officer to retire from the command of this Battalion without recording the sense he entertained of the value of his long and faithful services in the Militia of the Province, dating from the last War."

47. Alexander Macdonell (Aberchalder)—Major Lancaster (2nd) Regiment Glengarry Highlanders.

48. Donald Macdonell (Buidh)—Captain Lancaster (2nd) Regiment Glengarry Highlanders.

49. Alexander Macdonell (Lot No. 33, 6 con. Lancaster)—Ensign Lancaster (2nd) Regiment Glengarry Highlanders.

50. George Macdonell (of the family of Greenfield)—Captain Lancaster (2nd) Regiment Glengarry Highlanders.

51. Angus Macdonell (of the family of Greenfield)—Lieutenant Lancaster (2nd) Regiment Glengarry Highlanders.

52. Alexander Macdonell (of the family of Greenfield)—Ensign Lancaster (2nd) Regiment Glengarry Highlanders.

53. Ranald Macdonell—Captain Lancaster (2nd) Regiment Glengarry Highlanders.

54. John Allan Macdonell (styled Agent)—Ensign Lancaster (2nd) Regiment Glengarry Highlanders.

55. Donald Macdonell—Captain 3rd (Lochiel) Regiment Glengarry Militia.

56. Donald Macdonell—Lieutenant (3rd) Lochiel Regiment Glengarry Militia.

57. A. Macdonell—Lieutenant 1st (Charlottenburgh) Regiment Glengarry Militia. (Commission dated January 1, 1838).

58. A. Macdonell—Ensign 1st (Charlottenburgh) Regiment Glengarry Militia. (Commission dated January 1, 1838.)

59. Angus Macdonell—Colonel 4th (Kenyon) Regiment Glengarry Militia. (Commission dated 27 June, 1837.)

60. A. Macdonell—Lieut.-Col. 4th (Kenyon) Regiment Glengarry Militia. (Commission dated 18th October, 1837.)

61. A. Macdonell (Insh)—Major 4th (Kenyon) Regiment Glengarry Militia. (Commission dated 18 October, 1837.)

62. G. Macdonell—Captain 4th (Kenyon) Regiment Glengarry Militia. (Commission dated October 18, 1837.)

63. Neil Macdonell (Surveyor Indian Lands)—Captain 4th (Kenyon) Regiment Glengarry Militia. (Commission dated October 19, 1837.)

64. A. Macdonell—Captain 4th (Kenyon) Regiment Glengarry Militia. (Commission dated October 20, 1837.)

65. A. Macdonell—Lieutenant 4th (Kenyon) Regiment Glengarry Militia. (Commission dated October 18, 1837).

66. Donald Æneas Macdonell (of the family of Scothouse)—Lieut.-tenant-Colonel Stormont Regiment of Militia. (Commission dated January 28th, 1830). Had served as a volunteer in the Glengarry Light Infantry Regiment during War of 1812-14, and was afterwards a Lieutenant in the 98th [Royal Tipperary] Regiment. Member for Stormont in several Parliaments, and Warden Provincial Penitentiary, 1849-69.

67. J. Macdonell—Lieutenant-Colonel 1st Regiment Dundas Militia. [Commission dated April 29th, 1837].

68. J. Macdonell—Lieutenant-Colonel 2nd Regiment Dundas Militia. [Commission dated April 29th, 1837].

69. John Macdonell—Colonel Prescott Militia Regiment. [Commission dated April 1, 1822].

70. A. Macdonell—Lieutenant-Colonel Russell Regiment Militia. [Commission dated January 4th, 1838.]

71. A. Macdonell—Lieutenant-Colonel Northumberland Militia Regiment. [Commission dated January 5th, 1838].

72. A. Macdonell—Captain 1st Regiment Stormont Militia. [Commission dated January 14th, 1822].

73. R. Macdonell—Captain 1st Regiment Stormont Militia. [Commission dated May 26th, 1835].

74. A. Macdonell—Captain 1st Regiment Stormont Militia. [Commission dated February 1st, 1838].

75. R. Macdonell—Captain 1st Regiment Stormont Militia. [Commission dated February 1st, 1838].

76. J. Macdonell—Captain 1st Regiment Stormont Militia. [Commission dated December 26th, 1838].

77. A. Macdonell—Lieutenant 1st Regiment Stormont Militia [Commission dated November 9th, 1827].

78. A. Macdonell—Lieutenant 1st Regiment Stormont Militia. (Commission dated February 1st, 1838).

79. D. Macdonell — Lieutenant 1st Regiment Stormont Militia. (Commission dated February 1st, 1838).

80. J. Macdonell—Ensign 1st Regiment Stormont Militia. (Commission dated November 13th, 1827).

81. A. Macdonell—Ensign 1st Regiment Stormont Militia. (Commission dated May 26th, 1835).

82. A. Macdonell—Ensign 1st Regiment Stormont Militia. (Commission dated February 1st, 1838).

83. Alexander Macdonell (of the family of Greenfield)—Captain Glengarry Light Infantry Company (stationed at Coteau du Lac). For many years Colonel Dundas Militia.

84. Reginald Macdonell (of the family of Greenfield)—Ensign Glengarry Light Infantry Company. On Staff Colonel C. B.

Turner, K.H., Particular Service. Afterwards Lieutenant and Adjutant Royal Canadian Rifle Regiment until his death.

85. Æneas Macdonell (of the family of Greenfield)—Ensign Glengarry Light Infantry Company.

NOTE.—The Knoydart Macdonalds, who were Clansmen of Glengarry's, are not included in the above list for the reason that at this late date it is impossible to distinguish between them and others of a similar name belonging to other Clans, such as Clanranald, the Isles, Sleat, Glencoe, etc. Were it possible to enumerate them the list would be largely augmented.

APPENDIX C.

GRANTS OF LAND SECURED FROM THE CROWN FOR THE CATHOLIC CHURCH IN UPPER CANADA BY BISHOP MACDONELL,

FROM RECORDS OF CROWN LANDS DEPARTMENT.

Grantee : Reverend Alexander Macdonell, of Charlottenburgh—Location : Lots 10 in 7th Finch, 38 in 10th Lancaster, 29 in 4th Kingston, 50, 51 and half of 52 in the 2nd N.S.R.R. Charlottenburgh, 26 in the 3rd S.S. Dundas Street, Trafalgar—Date : March 15th, 1806.

Reverend Alexander Macdonell, of Charlottenburgh—Lots 214, 237, 245, 246 and 244 in Town of Kingston, known as Selma Park, now occupied by College, Cathedral and Palace—March 25th, 1806.

Donald Macdonell, John Cumming, Rev. A. Macdonell and Pierre Fortier, in trust for a Roman Catholic Chapel—One acre of land in the Town of Kingston, consisting of Lots 180, 207 and 243, together with Lots 247 and 248 ; Church built in 1808, under invocation of St. Columba—April 2nd, 1806.

Alexander Macdonell—Lot 5 North side of Dundas Street, York—December 11th, 1806.

Honourable J. Baby, A. McDonell, Rev. A. Macdonell and John Small, in trust for the congregation of the the Roman Catholic Church, for the purpose of erecting a Chapel—Lot 6 on corner of George and Duke Streets, on which now stands the De La Salle Institute—March 17th, 1806.

Alexander Macdonell, in trust for the inhabitants of Glengarry, for the purpose of establishing Schools therein—Town Lot 17, South side Third Street, in the Town of Cornwall—February 17th, 1816.

Right Reverend Alexander Macdonell—Lots East half 24 and Nos. 25, 26, 27, 29 and East part 30 in the 7th, and 31 in the 8th Fenelon—November 28th, 1826.

Right Reverend Alexander Macdonell—Block 24 in the Town of Niagara, formerly part of Military Reserve, 4 acres ; Church built by Very Reverend E. Gordon—May 3rd, 1832.

Honourable and Right Reverend Alexander Macdonell, Right Reverend Remigius Gaulin and Reverend Angus Macdonell—Lot 6 North Harvey Street, Perth, in trust for a Church, and a piece of land on South side of Craig Street for a Burial Ground ; Church built by Very Reverend John Macdonald—February 3rd, 1834.

Do.—Lot 17 in 10th, Northern Division of the Gore of Toronto, in trust for a Church—February 3rd, 1834.

Do.—15 acres of the Crown Reservation in the Township of Harwich (Town of Chatham), in trust for a Church, etc.—February 3rd, 1834.

Do.—Broken Lots 10, 11 and 13 in the 8th Adjala, in trust for a Church and Schoolhouse—February 3rd, 1834.

Do.—Lots 116 and 117 in 2nd Concession, East side of the Penetanguishene road. in the Township of Tiny, in trust, etc. —February 3rd, 1834.

Do.—Lots 1 and 2 South of Brock Street and West of George Street, Nos. 1 and 2 North of Hunter Street and West of George Street, No. 14 New Survey fronting Hunter Street, and Park Lot 6 in the Town of Peterborough, in trust, etc. ; present Church commenced by Reverend Mr. Butler—February 18th, 1834.

Do.—A lot of land on the late Military Reserve at Toronto, in trust for a Church and Presbytery; now occupied by St. Mary's Church and Presbytery, originally erected by Bishop Charbonnel—April 20th, 1837.

Do.—Lot 43 in Front upon the River St. Clair in the Township of Moore—April 10th, 1838.

Do —Lot 24 in the 1st Concession, South of road in Tyendenaga, in trust, etc.—August 18th, 1836.

Do.—Lots 1, 2, 3 and 4, North of First Street and South of Second Street, Trent, in trust, etc.—June 9th, 1836.

Do.—The block of land, situate North of Duke Street, South of Bond Street, West of Church Street and East of Mark Lane, containing two 83-100th acres in Town of London ; also ten acres of Lot No. 3 West of the Proof Line in Warncliffe Highway, Township of London—May 15th, 1837.

I sent to Sir John Macdonald the advance sheets of this little sketch of the life of Bishop Macdonell, knowing how kindly a regard he entertained for the memory of one whom it was in early life his privilege to know, and of whom I had often heard him speak in terms of highest approbation.

Sir John, in answering my letter, mentioned an anecdote of the Bishop which is well worth preserving. It is a tradition that it was told at one of the dinners of the Highland Society of London by an officer who had served in Canada in the War of 1812-14, in the presence of the Prince Regent and the Duke of York, and did the then Chaplain no harm in that quarter. Sir John states that he is unable at this late date to remember from whom he heard the anecdote, but thinks it was from the late Chief-Justice McLean or Mrs. Cumming of Kingston, a sister of the late Colonel Duncan Macdonell of Greenfield; from whom he mentions he gathered many a story connected with early times and events in Canada.

It is a well known fact that when Ogdensburg was taken on the 23rd February, 1813, by a British force composed principally of the Glengarry Light Infantry Regiment and Glengarry Militia under Colonel George Macdonell (familiarly known among the Highlanders as " Red George") the action was performed without the orders of Sir George Prevost, then commanding in Canada, and who had the same evening left Prescott en route for Kingston. There would be no use now in entering into the merits of the controversy which subsequently took place regarding this aspect of the affair or Sir George Prevost's despatches in connection with it or his alleged alteration of them, or the incorrectness of the account given in Alison's History. Suffice it that Ogdensburg was captured, four officers and seventy men made prisoners of war, both barracks, two armed schooners and two large gunboats burned, eleven pieces of cannon and all the marine, ordnance, commissariat and quartermaster-general's stores taken, and a large loss inflicted upon the Americans in killed and wounded.

As the Highlanders marched across the thin ice of the St. Lawrence to the attack, on one flank was the Chaplain with his Cross in his hand to urge on that portion of them which were of his way of thinking in matters of Faith, while on the other was a brave Presbyterian Minister, the Reverend Mr. Mackenzie, holding up the Bible as an encouragement to those of his persuasion. One of the Chaplain's flock felt somewhat nervous under fire and showed a disposition to fall to the rear. whereupon the Chaplain ordered him to stand fast ; but his orders were disobeyed. An example became immediately necessary, and then and there the Chaplain excommunicated him from the Church of his forefathers. It would have been better for the man to have faced the Yankees than the wrath of Maighster Alastair, when, the enemy being in front, his blood was up and the terrors of the Church were at his disposal !

www.ingramcontent.com/pod-product-compliance
Lightning Source LLC
Chambersburg PA
CBHW020045030726
47499CB00007B/2594